FIVE MINUTES

Nick Lucas

BEACHFRONT ENTERTAINMENT

Boca Raton, Florida

Got five minutes? Well good, here's what Nick Lucas' amazing *Five Minutes* is all about...

Todd Jones is a hotshot realtor in Fort Lauderdale, Florida. He's got a hot girlfriend, too. The trouble is that Todd is a real bad judge of character, especially his own. Todd's got himself tangled up worse than an old fishing line balled up in that long forgotten tackle box in the garage. Let's enumerate.

One of Todd's biggest clients is mad because the property Todd talked him into buying is underwater—literally. A screwy surfer dude with a recreational drug habit and a millionaire gun manufacturer for a father has got some not-so-friendly dealers on his tail. Todd's mother has shown up and wants to live with him. And she's brought her pet pig. And, oh, yeah, there's this little problem Todd is having with one of his best friends, Dr. Doug Freeman. Todd has been sleeping with Doug's wife. Okay, so maybe he shouldn't have. He'd be the first to admit that it may have been an error in judgment on his part. He is a bad judge of character, remember?

And that leads us to Todd Jones' biggest problem. Dr. Doug has found out about Todd's philandering and is aiming a pistol at Todd's forehead even as we speak. Todd has five minutes to live. Maybe less if his girlfriend finds out about his cheating ways.

Nick Lucas' FIVE MINUTES starts at a brisk boil and never lets up until the last sentence is laid down in this gripping comic thriller about a man whose life has taken a quick and nasty turn for the worse. And goes downhill from there...

Here's what the critics have to say about
Nick Lucas' *Five Minutes*!

"Debut novelist Lucas joins the growing list of Florida crime writers (Carl Hiaasen, Laurence Shames, Tim Dorsey) who mix capers with comedy...Readers will fall hard for this lovable loser as he struggles to stay alive while keeping his girlfriend from finding out what he is doing and his mom's pet pig from eating his stuff. Further adventures would be most welcome." BOOKLIST

"It's a comic thriller with a wacky plot... Todd Jones is a hotshot realtor in Fort Lauderdale, Florida with a hot girlfriend...All kinds of bad stuff happens to Todd, he tries to have Dr. Doug killed, he continues his affair with the Docs wife, loses his girlfriend and a bunch of other stuff. But in the end everything seems to work out. The last sentence in the book is extremely clever. The book is only 245 pages and is a quick read. I liked it." JUST PLUM CRAZY

"Five Minutes: A Comic Thriller is a darkly funny, rip-roaring novel about a fast-talking realtor who is quite possibly the world's worst judge of character. Hunted down by drug dealers, irate customers, a betrayed girlfriend and the husband of a married woman he had an affair with, he has five minutes to live at the opening of the story - perhaps more if he can persuade the angry husband not to point the gun at his head. Then again, perhaps not. Oh, and his mother has come to live with him and won't take no for an answer. A wildly frantic novel about a ne'er do well whose bad deeds have caught up with him, and his wacky struggle to stay just one step ahead of the trigger, suspenseful to the very last word." MIDWEST BOOK REVIEW

Look for these other great Beachfront Entertainment titles:

By Nick Lucas–

Twelve Hours (coming soon!)

By J.R. Ripley–

Tony Kozol mysteries:

Stiff In The Freezer

Skulls Of Sedona

Lost In Austin

Bum Rap In Branson

Gunfight In Gatlinburg

Gendarme Charles Trenet novels:

Murder In St. Barts

Death Of A Cheat

By Glenn Meganck–

After The Fall

George And The Angels

It's A Young, Young World

For Children–

Big Deal

Big Deal At The Center Of The Earth

No Big Deal

Aliens In The Greenhouse

By Marie Celine–

Lights, Camera, Death! (coming soon)

—Beachfront Entertainment—

Beachfront Entertainment - Correspond with Beachfront via email at: info@beachfrontentertainment.com

ISBN-13: 978-1494218362 /ISBN-10: 1494218364

Library of Congress CIP Data (Hardcover)

Lucas, Nick date

Five Minutes / Nick Lucas

1. Real estate agents – Fiction. 2. Fort Lauderdale (Fla.) – Fiction. 3. Adultery – Fiction. 4. Revenge – Fiction.

PS 3612.U245F58   2005   813'.6—dc22   2004063612

Cover Art by **RITA**

Five Minutes

:1

"You've got five minutes to live."

Todd chuckled. "Very funny, Doug."

Doug Freeman, good friend and general practitioner, had agreed to work Todd in as his last patient of the day. That made him a real good friend in Todd's book. He didn't have a lot of time to waste on doctor visits. The real estate market was hot right then and running his own office was running him down. Todd's girlfriend kept telling him that if he didn't slow down he was going to end up in his own special six feet of real estate.

Todd believed her. The thing was, real estate was hot now. Had he mentioned that? And that healthy six fig income it earned him every year softened the pain. Todd figured, if you do it up right—leather sofa, plasma screen TV, Bose home theater sound system, Sub-Zero fridge and a well-stocked wine cellar—even Hell could be quite livable.

Watching Doug stuff an x-ray into a manilla folder, Todd crossed his left foot over his right knee and cupped his hands

1

behind his head. Doug and one of his nurse assistants, Peg, had given him the once over. Needles, thermometers, pressure cuffs, little hammers. The works.

It was after six. Doug had sent Peg home and he and Todd were all snugly-like in his womb-like office on the fourth floor of the Fort Lauderdale Medical Arts Building in oh-so-beauteous Florida. Beat the hell out of freezing his tail off in Detroit, his hometown, at any rate.

"So, really," Todd said, "what's the deal? Have I got anything to worry about?" He'd been having these nagging chest pains the past couple of weeks or so. Nothing to fret about, he was sure. But still, figured he'd get it checked out. His girlfriend kept bugging him and was going to keep bugging him until he did.

That's the way Holly was. She could bug a guy to death. About the only current running stronger through Holly was her libido. Thank God for that.

Didn't hurt that she was a loan officer at Florida Sunshine Savings and Loan either. Having her there had greased a lot of wheels that otherwise wouldn't have turned—deals that would otherwise have died on the Todd Jones Realty office floor.

So here Todd was.

Doug wasn't smiling. And there was something in his eyes. Something unreadable. "Four minutes, forty-five seconds, Todd."

"Gee, doesn't give a guy much time, does it?" Todd sniffed. His nostrils stung. The scent of Doug's Giorgio cologne was being bested by the overpowering, omnipresent odor of Lysol antiseptic.

2

Doug shook his head. All the while, he never took his eyes off Todd; irises the color of hazelnut shells. Maybe it was because they looked so unshatterable and hard now that Todd thought of the nut analogy.

Todd suspected Doug was still pissed that he'd beat him by twelve strokes at golf the week before. Todd was hot.

What could he say?

He didn't make any excuses for his actions.

Todd sighed. "Come on, Doug. Cut the bullshit. I haven't got all day. If I've got something—some weird disease or a heart condition, just spill it. Otherwise," Todd made a show of rising from his chair, "I'm out of here."

Doug extended his wrist and tapped his watch. It was a Rolex, twenty grand if it was twenty cents. "Three minutes forty-seven seconds."

Todd was starting to get mad now. After all, Doug was his friend, but he could be a real pain sometimes. A real stick-in-the-mud, too. "Doug—"

"You fucked Caroline."

"What?" Todd said. The word spilled out in a laugh. "What are you talking about?" He shifted in his seat. Was it hot in here?

"You fucked my wife." Doug reached into a drawer, still without taking his eyes off Todd's (hazelnut brown vs. seagrape green—it wasn't much of a contest of wills), and when he brought out his hand, it held a gun. Todd didn't know much about guns but he knew enough to know that this thing was real. Doug carefully laid it on his desk.

Oh shit, thought Todd.

"You fucked my wife and now you have—" He looked at

that damn watch of his again. "Two minutes, twenty-nine seconds to live."

Todd's mind went into overdrive. Sonofabitch. He was serious. But would Doug really shoot him? Was that stinking thing even loaded?

What if he ran for the door? Could he possibly make it?

Maybe he could tip the desk over on him? Make his getaway then?

But that desk was big and heavy by the look of it. Doug was a successful doctor. He could afford the best. That desk was solid, sturdy. Unmovable.

Just my luck, thought Todd. He'd never be able to heave the monstrosity far enough or quickly enough. He did the next best thing.

In retrospect it was the next stupidest thing.

He dove for the gun. Todd went sliding and crashing over the desk, pencils and papers kicking up a storm, as his chair flew in the opposite direction.

Todd had to give Newton credit. Isaac was right about a few things and hadn't he said something about for every action there was an equal and opposite reaction?

Oh well. Even if Sir Newton was alive today, Todd realized, it seemed unlikely he'd get to ask the multi-talented maestro of math about that now.

Todd squeezed his eyes shut just for a second, just long enough to keep that wicked looking flying fountain pen coming his way from poking one of his eyeballs out.

When Todd looked up, the gray muzzle of that gun was looking at him like a cold, unblinking eye. Doug was staring at Todd with his own cold and dead looking dark eyes. His lips barely moved.

Doug's hand, finger on the trigger, barely quavered. "You fucked my wife and now I'm going to kill you, Todd. Is this really how you want to spend your last—" that damn Rolex again, "—minute and thirteen seconds?"

Todd's heart drummed so loudly he could feel Doug's desk quaking under him. He pushed backwards and fell to the ground.

Doug was still sitting there, smug and dangerous, in his high-backed leather swivel chair.

Todd pulled open the office door and stumbled down the narrow corridor, lined with insipid shots of bland scenery he had barely noticed before and wished he could leap into now, leading back to the waiting room. There was a painting of the Smoky Mountains, that Todd used to think insipid and derivative, that now looked damn near idyllic. The pains in his chest shot like arcs of lightning with each step.

Shit shit shit.

One thought ran over and over through Todd's addled mind like an unending loop of tape.

How had Doug found out?

:2

The first shot shattered the office door.

Todd didn't bother to survey the damage. He kept running. Elevator. Elevator. Twenty yards away. A woman in an unbuttoned lab coat and a wrinkled black skirt stepped into the open door.

"Hold the—" Todd's words came out in sobs. His lungs were nearly burst like two over-inflated balloons. Her eyes looked at Todd in frightened surprise as he headed for the safety of the elevator and her company. The woman in the lab coat heaved a visible sigh of relief as the doors closed in his face before he could make it to her side.

The elevator was gone.

Todd stopped to think but not for long. Footsteps, heavy running footsteps, pounded the floor. He knew Doug wasn't far behind him, though he couldn't see Doug from around the bend in the corridor.

Doug was a doctor, for crying out loud. Hadn't he taken some kind of oath about not killing his patients?

Decision time, realized Todd. It was try another office or

try the stairs. Another office might provide some sort of refuge. If anyone was still working. Doug wouldn't shoot him in front of witnesses, would he? Witnesses and coworkers who could certainly ID him in a line-up?

It was a chance Todd decided he couldn't risk. He grabbed the door handle to the stairs and wrenched it open. Todd literally fell down the first six or seven steps before realizing this was not the way to make progress.

And if Todd got hurt, he'd only end up in a hospital and that would be playing into Dr. Doug's evil, vengeful hands.

With a deep breath, Todd pulled himself up, allowed himself one guilty look at the door leading to the stairwell, then forced himself to take fast, yet methodical steps.

Todd had read once that some nut had made it all the way to the top of the Empire State Building in something like nine minutes flat. That was one hundred and two floors. One thousand, eight hundred and sixty steps! Todd figured he ought to make it down the three remaining flights to the Fort Lauderdale Medical Arts Building in about nine seconds.

After all, figured Todd, he may not have been in the best of shape but it was downhill and he had a loaded gun aiming for his coccyx for that extra little nudge of motivation. What had motivated that guy to run up to the top of the Empire State Building, for crying out loud?

Todd flew down the first couple flights of stairs then stopped dead in his tracks. A poor choice of words and Todd wished he hadn't said them even to himself.

The sound of Todd's sharp rasping cut through the still, hot air of the stairwell and echoed up and away as he considered his predicament. The movement of his lungs sounded like a couple of burly lumberjacks cutting through the belly of a forty-inch sequoia log right there under the stairs someplace with one of those long and wicked two-handled saws.

Todd was stuck in the stairwell, sequoia and all. Doug was above him or below him. He was a genius, right? Todd heard nothing from above. That meant a couple of things that came to his mind. There may have been other explanations and options that he would think of later, but he could only think of the two at the moment.

Todd quickly tossed out the nagging line of thought that told him that if he lived long enough to revisit his current situation he might realize there were other plausible possibilities. This was pointless. Because if he'd screwed up that bad, he wouldn't be alive to ponder the error of his ways.

He'd be dead.

The two possibilities that crossed his mind were that, number one, good old Doug was creeping down the stairs in his Mephistos. Damn things were comfy as walking on billowy clouds, quiet and silent. The second possibility was that Doug was already waiting for him downstairs.

There were two elevators. Doug could have come down in the second.

It was decision time.

Todd was not good at decisions. Took him six years out of college just to decide to go into real estate. Now, if a prospective buyer doesn't make an offer by the time he'd shown him or her their fourth property, he all but gave up on them as clients. He hated indecision in others. Probably because it reminded him of his own foible.

No more free rides on Todd's time.

So, Todd pondered, his heart thumping and his palms sweating, was he going to bail out on the second floor? Or should he head straight for the ground?

Todd tilted his head, straining to hear even the slightest sound from up in the stairwell. Please, give me something to help me make up my mind; to help me make the right, life-saving, choice prayed Todd.

But nothing came. Not a peep.

Then again, not a gunshot either. So there's always an upside to any situation, huh.

Todd had to admit, his first instinct was to keep running. Get to the lobby. Get out of the building. Get in his car.

AND GET THE HELL OUT OF HERE.

But that was probably just what Doug Freeman, M.D., was expecting. He knew Todd. He knew Todd was scared and he knew Todd would run like the quintessential scared rabbit.

Todd felt his hand shaking and his jaw clenching as he painfully, slowly edged open the stairwell door to the first floor.

A hiss of cool air, light as a woman's touch, brushed his leg, nearly gave him a stroke.

Todd regrouped and stuck his toe through the opening.

He'd rather lose a toe than a nose. Lose a toe, you might hobble a little. Lose a nose and you'd never stop to smell the roses again. And what about sex? What kind of women went for men without noses?

Nothing.

Todd cracked the door enough to get his head through.

The corridor, a mirror image of the floors above and below, was empty, quiet and still.

But Todd knew this floor would be like the others. The halls in this building were U-shaped. Doug could be lurking behind one of two possible corners.

Okay, Monty. Which will it be? Hall number one or hall number two?

:3

Todd backed up the stairs, stopping midway between floors two and three. Todd wasn't good at making decisions. Had he mentioned that?

But the higher Todd went the higher his fear rose, too. He backed down the stairs and faced the door leading out to the second floor. The handle was cool to his touch.

Todd's only hope was that Doug was as confused as he was. Todd's confusion was based on fear. Doug's confusion had at its base a foundation of mad rage, he supposed.

Hell. Todd hadn't realized Doug would get so mad over him screwing his wife. It was only the one time. Well, more than one, to be honest. A few times, that's all. Not so much.

Todd hadn't thought Doug would discover Caroline and his little indiscretion either. How had he found out? Hidden cameras? Detectives? Caroline squealed?

Caroline was good at squealing. Between the sheets, that is.

Without another thought, Todd yanked open the door.

There was a scream.

11

So Todd screamed, too.

The screaming woman in the hall, in a pale blue nurse's uniform, support hose and white sneakers, dropped her purse.

Todd bent down and picked it up for her. She screamed some more and whacked him in the face with her purse as he handed it to her. A twinge of pain and a warm gush of blood told Todd that the sharp-cornered brass buckle of her purse had split the inside of his lip as it pushed against his teeth.

She wound up for a second swing and Todd dodged.

"Hey! Stop it!" Todd held out my hands. "Cut it out!"

"Pervert! Thief!" She kicked him in the shin and bolted as the elevator doors swung open. Hopping on one foot, Todd could see four others inside, all medical personnel by the look of them, done for the day. Heading home, a little dinner, a little TV. Maybe a drink or two.

Todd could've used a drink about then. But this girl was yelling and pointing up the hall at him. Todd dropped his injured leg and made himself look as harmless as possible under the circumstances (smile for the camera, Todd) but everybody's eyes were growing dark and accusing. One heavy looking thug balled up his hands into fists.

Todd turned and headed back down the stairs.

Ground floor. It might as well have been Ground Zero.

Somewhere out there in the Florida sun was Todd's car. His escape route. His freedom.

All Todd had to do was get through the lobby and out those doors.

Without getting shot.

Todd peered through the tiny glass window of the

stairwell door. The ugly crowd from the elevator, including that girl that slugged him, were pouring out of the elevator and heading outdoors. Todd thought briefly about joining them, safety in numbers and all that, but decided those numbers were not on his side.

If he tried to join up with that mob, they'd probably turn on him and pound him to the ground like a half-kilo of cheap sausage. Even a quick shot was preferable to that. Less painful. Boom! Goodnight.

Todd waited till they'd all filed outside and gave them an extra few seconds to be on their respective ways.

There was no sign of Doug.

The door gave with a squeak. Just his luck. What kind of a building was this, anyway? With the money they charged per square foot, didn't they have somebody to oil squeaky doors?

Keeping the door in front of him like a giant mediaeval shield, Todd scouted out the lobby. The coast looked clear and that was good enough for him.

Todd bolted to the door and pushed his way to freedom. It was a hot summer evening and Florida let him know it in no uncertain terms. And the doors faced south. Full frontal Florida sunshine flexed her muscles and slapped him.

But he didn't let it slow him down. Todd's car was on the right in the far parking lot. There were a few people in the lot, but no sign of Doug. So far, so good.

There she was, Todd's silver BMW, with the blue leather interior. Last year's model. He had a thirty-nine month lease. It was the 540i model. Not one of those new 760Li's. Too fancy, and too deep for his pockets. Doug's wife, Caroline, had one though. She gushed over hers.

Personally, Todd liked the 760Li's backseat. They'd used that at the beach once up near Boca. Nothing like living a little dangerously. Nothing like getting naked on fine leather.

Todd dug his hands deep into his trousers. The look on his face as reflected in his lovely BMW's clean safety glass said it all.

No keys.

Todd's mind race like he wished the BMW's engine was then. Keys. Keys. Who's got the keys?

With a groan, Todd remembered that his key ring was in his sportcoat and he'd taken that off in Doug's office. Todd's wallet was in that coat, too. He patted his back pockets to make sure. Yep. In the examination room. Along with his cellphone. Todd gazed up at the peach-colored medical arts building and swore.

He was going to have to go back.

:4

Todd chewed his lip a moment. Go back. The words, even as he repeated them in his head, sounded both stupid and necessary.

Taking a deep breath and looking both ways, he slouched forward and loped back towards the medical arts building. Was that dark shadow he spotted at that fourth floor window Doug Freeman? Private enemy number one?

He pushed the button for the elevators. The one on the left swung open with a nearly silent rumble. Todd stepped inside.

But he felt uneasy there. Boxed in. No air. No escape. What if Doug was standing on the other side when the doors opened again? He wouldn't stand a chance.

Before the elevator could lift off, he thrust out his hand and the doors reopened. Entering the stairwell, he climbed slowly. Pausing at every landing and listening for the sounds of approaching steps.

But he was alone.

Mercifully.

Wandering on tiptoes through Doug's deserted waiting room, Todd couldn't stop shaking. So this was what it was like to infiltrate enemy territory. If he hadn't been scared shitless, he'd have been exhilarated.

There was that painting of the Smoky Mountains once again. Maybe when this was all over he'd rent a little cabin up in Tennessee or North Carolina for a week. Better yet, buy one. He could keep it for himself a few weeks a year and rent it out to vacationers the remaining weeks. It'd pay for itself in no time.

The realtor in him stopped along with the rest of him. He could hear voices, or rather, a voice. Todd held his breath and listened. The sound came from Doug's office. Judging from the monolog, Todd figured Doug was on the phone.

Doug's office was up the hall and just around the corner. The examination room where Todd had left his jacket was to the left behind the unopened door. This was too easy.

Todd smiled.

"No, I haven't forgotten, dear. I have a little unfinished business here at the office," Doug said. There was a short pause. "I know that's what I always say, Caroline. That's because it's always true."

Todd rolled his eyes. Sounded like Caroline could be a real bitch. He was glad he was screwing her and not living with her.

With old Dougie-boy busy, Todd pushed open the door to the examination room. His jacket hung on the rack beside the examination table where he'd ignominiously allowed himself to be poked and prodded by that assistant of Doug's and then the great man himself.

FIVE MINUTES

He patted his pockets. Cellphone. Keys.

Yep, this was too easy. Todd tossed his jacket casually over his shoulder. If only he carried a gun. Packed a little heat. He'd give his ex-friend Doug Freeman a taste of his own medicine. *You've got ten seconds to live, Dougie-boy. How do you like that? Bang. Bang.*

There would be none of this five minute bullshit from him. Just plow Doug down. Be done with it. No Mr. Nice Guy bullshit. A guy could do a lot in five minutes. He had, hadn't he?

The door swung shut and Todd turned towards Doug's office, giving him the official one-finger salute. He turned and tiptoed towards the exit.

The phone went off in his pocket like a sonic rocket. AT&T's somewhat lackluster version of Scott Joplin's 'The Entertainer.' There was certainly nothing entertaining about that tune right then.

At that moment, the ringing phone blared like the Liberty Bell announcing a new British invasion to Todd's frightened ears and it had taken all his self-control to keep from hitting the ground as if a fellow GI had shouted 'Incoming!'.

If he hit the ground he'd have to get up again and that would only slow him down. Running forward and pawing his jacket, Todd snatched the phone from his pocket. Tripping on the outer office carpet, the phone flew from his hand as he extended a finger to hit the 'power off' button. The phone hit the wall and exploded. Its battery bounced off a waiting room chair and landed in the magazines.

At least the damn thing had stopped ringing.

Todd heard a hideous laugh and turned, one hand

17

holding the doorknob as if it was a life preserver. "Doug!"

Doug's lips and face were purple with rage. The gun waved in front of Todd like a living beast waiting to strike.

"Times up, Todd."

Todd threw up his hands. Why? Would they stop a bullet?

"Hey, Doug, old buddy—" Todd's mouth contorted into something resembling a smile. "Can't we work something—"

Doug's beeper went off and the doctor's gaze instinctively dropped to his belt where the beeper was clipped. Todd took this heavenly sent opportunity to yank the office door open. He ducked and lunged, pulling the door shut behind him. He heard Doug screaming obscenities even as he hit the ground on his shoulder, tumbled and rolled into a canvas-sided cart.

He looked up. A heavy-set woman in a dark blue uniform was yelling at him in some language he couldn't quite make out. Was she Haitian? Right skin tone.

Doug's door flew open. Seeing the cleaning woman, he thrust his gun inside his jacket and grinned. "Everything all right here?"

The cleaning woman pointed at Todd and rattled on for about thirty-seconds. Doug nodded.

Todd wondered if Doug even understood what the woman was saying. Todd didn't. But he loved the woman anyway. According to the plastic name tag pinned to her chest, her name was Odetta. And Todd was going to marry her. Marry her and bear her children.

She'd saved his life.

Todd picked himself up and dusted himself off. "Just a little accident. Nothing broken." Todd could see the cold bulge of the gun under Doug's jacket.

Doug nodded once more, squeezed his fingers together.

Todd smiled. Lots of teeth. If Doug was waiting for him to leave, to separate himself from Odetta, the doctor was out of luck. Todd planned on sticking with Odetta all night if he had to. Hell, he'd clean toilets if he had to.

Doug retreated to his office. But he returned a minute later clutching a briefcase. Doug said goodnight and Todd waved. The cleaning woman looked at them both then went about her business.

Todd heard the sound of an elevator opening and closing. But he was taking no chances. Doug could be standing right around the corner, gun in hand, just waiting for Todd to turn the bend. . .and BLAM! Right between the eyes!

Todd grabbed a rag and a bottle of window cleaner from Odetta's cart and followed her into the office across the hall. Dr. Dunbar, OB/GYN.

She looked scared at first and then rolled her eyes as Todd attacked the pane of glass separating the waiting room from the back office.

Todd was wiping the crud off a mirrored medicine cabinet in the hall restroom while Odetta attacked the toilet when a partial eclipse blocked the bathroom door.

Todd turned and found himself confronted with an enormous black man in a blue uniform much like Odetta's own, only his barely contained him and bulged in every direction. It was only a matter of time until the whole uniform exploded in a blue nova and Nelson, as read his nametag, would be producing eclipses in his skivvies.

Todd lowered the glass cleaning spray bottle that he'd

been aiming towards Nelson as if it was going to save him somehow. Had he really been thinking he was going to rub the guy out with ammonia water and a rag?

Not that Nelson had said or done anything particularly threatening, but there was something unreadable in his round, dark eyes that Todd found disturbing.

"Whatchou doin'?" The big guy's voice was higher pitched than Todd expected, higher even that Odetta's. Not that she was any songbird. He had a coarse stubble of salt and pepper hair across his jowls. A damp rag was hanging from his belt.

Todd cleared his throat and held up his spray bottle. "Helping out?"

"You gotta leave."

Todd glanced at Odetta. She was standing with her arms folded under her breasts. She didn't appear to be taking his side. "Odetta says you's botherin' her."

So that was what Odetta had been whispering about on the phone in the doctor's private office a few minutes ago. Here he thought she'd only been placing a few free long distance calls to her folks back home.

Todd stepped forward, but not far. Nelson was blocking the door. "Listen, Nelson?" The big guy nodded. "I really don't mind staying and I don't need any pay. In fact, I'd be happy to pay you. Pay you both—"

Nelson's Chihuahua-sized hands came down on Todd's bony shoulders. "You's gotta leave."

"Go on, fool!" Odetta chimed in.

Todd studied the giant. He was big, big enough to be a tackle. One of those big Green Bay Packer guys. Layers of fat covering layers of muscle. Todd could be squished like the proverbial bug.

Then again, Doug could be waiting just about anywhere. Doug had had plenty of time to lay an ambush. Todd wouldn't stand a chance. All in all, Todd liked his chances better with Odetta and Nelson.

Todd took a deep breath. "No."

Nelson's right eyebrow shot up. His forehead transformed into a sea of deep wrinkles. Todd figured no one had ever said no to the big guy before—at least and lived—and he didn't know how to take it. He'd been caught off guard.

But Nelson's confusion was short-lived. He picked Todd up by his armpits, carried him to the hall and threw him down.

Todd jumped up, looking over his shoulder for Doug in case the lunatic was waiting around the corner and decided to come out firing. Nelson stood in the doorway. Todd shot past him and to the doctor's private office. He held onto the doorframe with both hands.

Nelson came stomping in after him. "What you, crazy?"

Todd was trembling. Nelson could beat him to a pulp any minute. Why the hell hadn't he used that Bally's gym membership he'd bought two years ago? Muscles money down the drain. "Listen, Nelson. I don't want any trouble. I just don't want to leave."

Todd steadied himself. "If you want me to leave this building," Todd began, knowing that this was the tricky part, "you're going to have to carry me out."

Nelson's eyes beaded up. So did his hands. Into fists the

size of softballs.

Odetta was watching from the restroom door. Nelson looked at her as if looking for answers. She complied. "Get that fool out of here, Nelson. I got me work to do."

Nelson shrugged and planted his feet in front of Todd. Todd didn't plan on offering any resistance. He wanted Nelson to drag him out to his car conscious, not comatose.

Nelson hoisted Todd by the waist, squeezing the breath out of him. As the big man tossed him over his shoulder, Todd waved goodbye to Odetta. "It's been a pleasure."

Odetta rolled her eyes and turned her back

.

:5

Todd winced as his head bumped off the metal doorframe of the main entrance. "You're a little rough with the merchandise, aren't you there, Nelson?"

Nelson grunted. Nelson was more than a little rough with the merchandise and didn't seem to mind. At least the burly man had relaxed his grip enough so that Todd could breathe. For a while there, Todd thought he was going to pass out from asphyxiation before they even got out of the elevator. Todd rubbed his scalp with one hand and swiveled his neck around. Doug's speed yellow Porsche sat in the parking lot. Doug was behind the wheel. Dark glasses, despite the twilight, covered his eyes.

Todd flashed Doug a grin and waved. Even from a distance, Todd noticed Doug's hands wrap around his steering wheel in a grip of death.

"Tough shit, Dougie," he muttered.

"Whatchou say?"

"Thinking out loud. That's all." Todd sensed that Nelson was about to lower him to the ground. That wouldn't do.

Wouldn't do at all. As soon as Nelson got inside, Doug could whirl up and blow him away. "Hey, what do you know. I think I forgot something upstairs. Thanks for the lift, Nelson, old buddy. But I can handle things from here."

Nelson squeezed Todd's waist. "You ain't goin' back inside. Where's you car?"

Todd sighed. His hands flopped. He pointed and the big guy dropped him at his door. "Now that's curb service." Todd laughed. Nelson didn't.

"Get in."

Todd noticed his hands were shaking. Still, he managed to unlock and get the key in the ignition.

Nelson's thick fingers held onto the driver's side window. He was going to get smudges everywhere and the car had just been washed, but Todd figured it best not to complain. He did wish he'd kept his spray bottle and rag though.

"Nice wheels."

"Thanks."

"Start her up and don'tchou come back."

Todd nodded. So much for Southern hospitality.

As he hit Broward Boulevard, one of Fort Lauderdale's main thoroughfares, Todd noticed Doug's Porsche 911 right behind him. Not that Todd was any Sherlock Holmes. But it would have been pretty hard to miss a bright yellow sports car being driven by a homicidal maniac.

Todd clenched his teeth. It seemed old friend Doug wasn't ready to let go of this thing yet. It seemed to Todd that Doug was awfully touchy on the subject of marital fidelity. What harm was there in a little fling now and then? Doug wasn't exactly Mr. Straight Arrow himself. Todd had heard the stories. Doctors attracted women, from cute little staffers to frisky patients.

Why was Doug making such a big deal out of this?

Todd jumped into traffic just ahead of a slow-moving city bus. The bus driver laid on his horn and Todd waved. Doug hadn't made the turn, but Todd had no doubt he wasn't going to stop this wicked game now.

Getting rid of Doug was going to take some doing, more than cutting in front of one stinking city bus. But Todd knew every street in Ft. Lauderdale. It was his job. He was out here every day. While Doug was locked away in his office or in some hospital someplace ripping open people's guts with one hand while his other hand ripped one hundred dollar bills from their billfolds.

Doug may know flesh and blood, but the streets were Todd's domain. Porsche or no Porsche, Todd wasn't going to lose this race, not if his life depended on it.

Which it unfortunately did.

Todd swung the wheel hard, ignoring the Right Turn On Red After Stopping sign and plowed on. He wanted to get over to Las Olas Boulevard. This time of day, traffic would be heavy but there'd be plenty of people about. Plenty of witnesses.

He caught a flash of yellow in the rearview mirror and knew that Doug had spotted him. Todd stepped on the gas, ran another red light and dodged nimbly around a Jeep Wrangler that couldn't seem to make up its mind if it was driving or parking.

The driver of the Chevy in front of Todd wasn't so cooperative and seemed to be driving as slow as he could merely to annoy him. Todd honked three times and shot the driver the finger twice. Still no progress.

Didn't this guy understand Todd's testosterone-based sounds and hand signs? What kind of a man was he?

The William Tell Overture interrupted his thoughts. "What?" screeched Todd, yanking loose his car phone. Who the hell was bothering him now? "I'm kind of busy here. I'll call you back later." Todd pulled the phone from his ear and honked at some idiot on a bike who kept drifting into traffic. Nonetheless, the voice on the other end of the line made itself heard loud and clear.

"Todd, this is Aristotle Constantine."

Shit. "Hello, Mr. Constantine," said Todd, desperately trying to maintain his calm. "How are you, sir?"

"I've been trying to reach you for hours. What the hell have you been doing?"

"Sorry, Mr. Constantine," said Todd. "I had a doctor's appointment."

"You don't keep me happy," warned Constantine, "you're gonna need another doctor's appointment.

Todd swallowed hard. "Yes, sir." Mr. Constantine was a man whose business Todd very carefully tried not to know. Constantine had money and he had muscle. Both of which he liked to flex. Todd had had several business deals with the man and they'd both made some big money.

"Peter tells me those lots you sold me up in Boca are underwater."

Todd gripped the wheel with one hand and slowed to match the barely moving traffic. "Don't worry about it, Mr. Constantine," said Todd with a voice like butter wrapped in silk. This is Florida," Todd managed to say with a tone of nonchalance that he wasn't exactly feeling, "everything is underwater."

Constantine was a humorless man and replied with a chorus of invectives.

"We'll work it out, Mr. Constantine, I promise. We'll pump it out. It's only water." Todd cursed a delivery truck that was half-blocking the lane. "Those lots are going to be worth millions once we develop them."

Todd's agency had sold Constantine four submerged lots along the Intracoastal Waterway in Boca Raton. He had told Constantine those lots were going to need some developing before they could be built on. What was the guy getting so excited about? Jesus. Everybody was so touchy these days.

Todd strung out several assurances and Constantine returned the volley with a number of painful sounding promises of his own if things didn't work out in his favor and to his liking. Finally, the assurances won out and Constantine cut the connection.

Todd threw the phone across the seat and slammed his fist against the console. "FUCK!"

Approaching a signal-less intersection, Todd angrily accelerated, hoping to pass the moron in front of him. A car coming from the other direction forced him to pull back. Todd was compelled to slam on his brakes when the Chevy stopped dead in the street.

A jowly, pale faced man with a salt and pepper crewcut thrust his head out the window of the Chevy and assailed Todd. "What's the hurry, buddy?" He had a deep, cavernous voice but actually appeared quite placid.

"Fuck off!" Todd was an excellent debater.

The Chevy driver's brow shot up. "You have some sort of problem? Is there an emergency of some sort?" His voice remained level beyond all reason.

Todd growled. Traffic was backing up all around. Pedestrians shot nervous glances at their two vehicles. He had to get moving. "What is it about fuck and off that you don't understand?"

The Chevy driver's arm withdrew into his car and Todd hoped he was about to put his drab looking sedan in gear. Of course, the idiot could be reaching for a weapon. Just what Todd needed, another homicidal maniac looking to gun him down. Well, if this guy wanted a shot at him, he'd better hurry up about it, because once Doug caught up with them he was going to lose his only chance.

Instead, the arm reappeared. The man's hand held a brown leather wallet which he carefully opened and pointed at Todd.

Todd had to unlatch his seatbelt and stick his head out the window to get a good look. Some sort of ID, too tiny to read from a distance. But that big, shiny badge, that was hard to miss. "You're a cop?" His mouth was suddenly dry as four ounces of Sahara straight up.

Todd cursed his luck. He didn't feel so good. His stomach got that queasy, nervous feeling he experienced whenever he braved one of those high-speed roller coaster rides—which wasn't too often. He hated that feeling.

Todd didn't want any cops, either, even with Doug after him. Doug knew too many of his secrets. Knew about the questionable land deals and the offshore money laundering for all the wrong kinds of people. Shit shit shit.

If he got the police involved in his little problem with Doug, the police might start looking into him as well. Maybe even the IRS. Better Doug than those guys.

Besides, Todd was certain that he and Doug could still work this out. At the very least, Doug would get tired of taking potshots at him and give it up. Todd would buy a round of drinks. One day the two men would laugh about this whole thing over a Sunday barbecue. *Hey, Doug, remember that year I was sleeping with your wife? Wasn't that a hoot? You chasing me with that gun and all. Yeah, boy, those were good times all right. . .*

Yet first Todd had to get rid of the policeman. But how?

Todd fell back into his seat. A fresh line of perspiration clung to his upper lip like a leech.

The wallet snapped shut. "How about you follow me up to the next street and pullover."

Todd would have answered no, but it most definitely had been a statement, not a question. This wasn't going to be good. Then again...

Todd glanced in his mirror. The Porsche was visible about four cars back, stuck in the traffic jam that he and Mr. Chevy had created. Having a cop for company could be almost as good as keeping company with his old buddy Nelson the maintenance man. Doug wouldn't dare stick around while Mr. Chevy wrote him out a ticket.

Todd smiled and waved Mr. Chevy on ahead. His luck was holding after all.

:6

Todd stepped out of his car with only a moment's hesitation. That moment of hesitation came as he realized that it was only the car that stood between him and a bullet. In the open, he'd be a sitting duck. If Doug decided to go duck hunting, that is. The question was: would Doug be crazy enough to take a shot at him out here? In front of a cop? Was he mad enough?

Todd and the officer had pulled into the back lot of a restaurant behind Las Olas Boulevard. There wasn't much for cover besides more vehicles. The Porsche came slowly up the side street. Doug's two hands were on the wheel.

Todd breathed a sigh of relief. Unless Doug had surgically attached or suddenly grown a third arm, that left no arm for shooting. Todd twisted his own right hand into the shape of a gun—thumb up, index finger out—and aimed at Doug as he passed. "Pow."

Doug's stony face remained unmoved. But Todd could just imagine what the bastard was thinking.

A tap on the shoulder from behind sent Todd reeling. Mr.

Chevy caught him. Todd was just under six foot. This guy was just under him. He looked to be in his late thirties and was just about that many pounds overweight. He had a pug nose with large skin pores. A lone brown mole clung to his left ear like a walnut-shaped earring.

"You sure you're okay?"

Todd nodded.

"You don't look okay." The man's eyebrows wiggled and Todd squirmed as the man's eyes burrowed under his skin. "You look kind of—" Mr. Chevy paused, "—frazzled."

Frazzled? Todd frowned. "Look, it's been a long day. How about you write me up a ticket and we both call it a day."

This made Mr. Chevy smile. "I don't do tickets."

Todd's head twisted to one side. "You don't do tickets." What the hell was that supposed to mean? What was with this guy? Was everybody he was going to run into today going to be crazy?

Was there a full moon tonight?

Mr. Chevy shook his head and retrieved his wallet. He stuck it in Todd's face, so close that Todd could smell the cheap cowhide. "I'm a detective. Broward County."

Todd backed away to read the print on his ID. Nicholas Durham, Detective. Broward County Sheriff's Dept. What the hell?

The detective shoved the wallet back in his rear pocket.

"Mind if I call you Nick? Ni-ni-ni-ni-ni-ni-ni-ni-ni-nick-e-lo-de-on!" Todd smiled. Durham didn't. Tough crowd today. Todd cleared his throat. "Okay, Det. Durham it is." Todd crossed his arms. "What can I do for you, detective?"

Det. Durham stuck his hands down his front pockets. His knees were bent and his chinos sagged as if he was already tired of standing. "Slow down. Lay off the horn. Take it easy."

Todd opened his mouth to reply but the detective cut him off. "You got some ID?"

Todd produced his wallet. It wasn't a bad picture but it wasn't his best. The idiot at the DMV had caught him mid-blink.

"Todd Jones?"

"In the flesh."

"If you want to stay in the flesh I suggest you drive more carefully in the future."

The detective rubbed the side of the billfold. "What is this stuff? Snakeskin?"

Todd shook his head. "Alligator."

"Must've cost you." Durham handed back the wallet. "A serious accident could cost you more."

Todd nodded. "Yes, sir." He ran a hand through his hair. "I don't know what got into me. Lots of stress at the office. You know how it is."

Durham nodded. "What do you do for a living, Mr. Jones?"

"Real estate."

Durham chuckled. "I should have known. Seems like everybody's selling everybody else a house in South Florida."

"Tell me about it," declared Todd. "The competition's tough. Damn tough."

"I'll bet." Durham looked off into the distance.

Todd took this opportunity to check his back. The

Porsche eased by.

Durham must have seen him looking. "Nice car," said the detective.

"Yeah, nice," agreed Todd.

"Wouldn't mind having a Porsche like that myself one day. Not that I'll ever be able to afford to on my salary."

"They don't come cheap."

"How much you think a car like that's worth?"

Todd shrugged. "Eighty-ninety grand." Doug had double-parked across the intersection. His car was a yellow droplet left behind by the setting sun. A complex and inviting mélange of scents from the French restaurant up the block wafted past, carried on the breeze pushing up from the ocean only a mile or two to the east.

Durham whistled. "Out of my league, all right." The detective turned to go. "You have a nice night, Mr. Jones."

Todd swallowed hard. It was nice having a bodyguard around, especially with Doug so near at hand. "Do you have any plans?"

Durham turned. "Plans?"

"Yeah. You doing anything?" Todd flashed his best and warmest salesman's smile. Took him hours of practice in front of the mirror to get that oh-so-sincere look. The smile had to look like it came up from the soul and spilled out over the lips and through the eyes.

Durham shrugged. "Nothing special."

"Can I buy you a drink?"

Det. Durham pinched his upper lip between his thumb and index finger for a moment before answering. "Couldn't hurt."

:7

The two men found spots for their respective cars and hoofed it over to Danny Boy's, a popular pub on Las Olas. Before going in, Todd shot a look outside for Doug. The Porsche was still where he'd last seen it, but there was no sign of its driver.

They dropped onto a couple of stools at the bar which was manned by a decidedly Nordic looking knockout with yellow hair that fell to taut and tanned cleavage. A black skirt and frilly white blouse completed the look. She flashed a pair of brilliant green eyes at Todd and Det. Durham. Words weren't necessary.

"I'll have a Red." Todd drummed his fingers on the heavily varnished bar.

"Red?" Durham asked.

"Murphy's Irish Red," Todd replied. He turned his lusty gaze away from the barmaid. "Great stuff." Durham appeared hesitant. "Try it."

Durham shrugged. He seemed to be big on shrugging and the young lady returned with two glasses of red stout.

Todd held up his glass. "To staying alive."

"Funny toast." Nonetheless, Det. Durham hoisted his mug and drank. "To staying alive."

They made small talk over their first beer. A Marlins vs. Braves game ran soundlessly on the TV in the corner. Durham said the Marlins stank. "Like yesterday's fish."

Todd laughed. The alcohol was helping him unwind, forget his immediate and life threatening troubles. "Thanks, Patty," he said as the bartender brought them another round. They were on a first name basis now.

As she turned away, both men stared. Long legs, trim behind. Just the kind of woman to make you spend your money. The guy who ran Danny Boy's was no fool, that was for sure, reasoned Todd.

"She likes you," said Durham, wiping his mouth with the side of his hand.

"You think so?"

Durham took a swallow and nodded. "I know people."

Todd cocked his head. Patty was leaning over the ice machine filling a blender, her skirt pulled tight across her rear. "She's a beauty all right." He sighed and turned back to the detective. "So what's your story?"

"Story?"

"Yeah." Todd ran a finger along the edge of his mug. "You married? Single? What?"

Durham stared into space, his eyes raking over the bottles against the back wall of the bar. "Married," he said finally. "Isn't everybody?"

"Not me," said Todd.

Durham's eyes grew wider. "Never?"

Todd shook his head firmly. "Never."

"Wow. That's something." He leaned closer. "How old are you?"

"You saw my license."

"I wasn't paying that close attention."

"Thirty."

Durham repeated. "Thirty." He drained his glass and called for another. "Hell, when I was thirty I'd already been married five fucking years."

Todd frowned. Things were not going as planned. Durham was dark and morose. The last thing in the world that Todd wanted now was to be some guy's shrink. And Durham was starting to look like a heavy drinker. That wasn't good. That could screw up everything.

Walking up to the pub, Todd had come up with the brilliant plan of getting drunk enough or, at the least, appearing drunk enough to the detective that the guy would escort him home. That would prevent Psycho Doug from popping him along the way. "How old are you now?"

"Thirty-seven." Durham pulled a bent pack of chewing gum from his pants and offered Todd a stick.

Todd declined. Spearmint chewing gum and stout? Not a pleasant combination. "Any kids?"

"Nah. Wife and I decided we didn't want any." The detective paused, stuffed his gum into his cheek and polished off his second beer. "Leastwise, she tells me that's what we decided."

"That's tough, Nick."

"I prefer Nicholas," said the detective, his unfocused eyes falling on Todd's nose. "As in Jolly Ole Saint Nicholas."

Todd quickly turned away and his eyes followed Patty as she delivered a round of ales to a small table at the window. She was getting lovelier by the minute. Patty caught him looking and smiled. The corners of her eyes got all crinkly and Todd suddenly wished he was flying solo instead of dragging around the anchor that was Det. Not-so Jolly Ole St. Nicholas Durham.

And Todd hadn't wanted to crack up laughing in front of Det. Durham. Jolly Ole St. Nicholas? Him? Who on earth was he trying to kid? Himself? Todd had seen jollier people at funerals.

"Got a girlfriend?"

Todd swiveled. "What?" He'd seen a dark shadow sitting on a bench across the street. It looked like Doug. Todd's pulse rate shot upward. He squinted and leaned closer as a line of cars went past. When Todd looked again, the shadowy figure was gone. Jesus, Doug had had a clean shot at him there. He needed to get out of the line of the open doorway. Durham's words finally sunk in. "Yeah. Name's Holly."

"She beautiful?"

Todd nodded, one eye on Durham, the other on the door.

"Beautiful as Patty here?"

Todd nodded some more. "Oh, yeah."

"Lucky bastard."

"I guess so." Except for that nagging little fly that was trying to kill him, Todd supposed he did have it pretty good, at least compared to Durham. "You hungry?"

Durham patted his belly. "I could eat."

"Great." Todd jumped down from his barstool. "There's

a table open in the corner. Let's jump on it."

"What's wrong with the bar?"

"Table's better."

"Better for what?" The detective seemed to almost involuntarily slide off his own leather capped stool.

Todd ignored Durham's question and grabbed a seat at the small table for two in the far corner nearest the restrooms. Todd took the chair facing the door, leaving Durham facing the sign to the men's room.

They ordered the whiskey chicken, an Irish specialty with plenty of onions, mushrooms, crème fraiche and, of course, a cup of Irish whiskey thrown in, and a pitcher of stout to wash it down their gullets.

Durham actually turned out to be an okay sort of guy once he'd loosened up. He had a number of amusing, if sick, stories about cases he'd worked on. Like the one he swore was true about the looser who'd robbed a Krispy Kreme donut shop. They'd nabbed the guy approximately two blocks away, but he escaped from the squad car. The perp literally jumped out of the moving car only to get run over in the street by a Krispy Kreme delivery van. "Divine justice," the detective stated.

Todd wasn't so sure about that, but he decided then and there not to step in front of any donut deliver vans no matter how long he lived or what he was running from at the time.

It was after eleven when Durham said he had to go and they got their alcohol-filled carcasses up from the table. Todd smiled when the detective insisted on following him home.

"You're drunk," said Durham.

"Not half as drunk as you, Ni-ni-ni-ni-ni-ni-ni-ni-ni-

Nickelodeon." Todd tottered as they stepped outside. Doug was a mere cloud in the back corners of his mind now.

"Just stick close." Durham helped Todd find his car and climb behind the wheel. "I'd hate to see you get a ticket."

Todd snickered. "You don't do tickets."

"No," said Durham, "but other cops do. How far's your place?"

"Port Lauderdale. It's a condo."

"I know the place."

Todd watched as the detective staggered off to his own vehicle. His plan had worked too well.

Todd was drunk. That made him vulnerable. He locked his doors. A wave of paranoia crept over him. It was dark back here in the parking lot. He and Durham were the only people around.

Would Doug kill him here? Would he kill Durham as well?

Was that a tree or something moving in the shadows? Todd felt his throat tighten up. The whole world was tightening up around him. Squeezing the breath, the life out of him.

Durham honked. Todd breathed a sigh of relief as the detective honked and motioned for Todd to get moving. Before long the tall, glittering lights of home, Port Lauderdale, one of Ft. Lauderdale's newest and ritziest condominiums sprang into view.

Todd pulled up to the valet and waved. Durham pulled up behind him.

"Have a good evening, Mr. Jones?" The valet was older than Todd, about forty or so and a good guy with two kids and a wife. Used to work for Enron or something. Life was a bitch.

"The best," Todd replied.

"Will you be needing your car again tonight?"

Todd said he wouldn't and sauntered over to the detective's car and laid his torso over the roof.

"Nice place." Durham's eyes climbed the crenellated heights.

"Wait till you see the view."

Durham shook his head. "Another time. I really should be getting back."

"Come on," drawled Todd, lazily, "only take a minute. We'll jump on the elevator and whoosh!" His hand shot up like a rocket. "Twenty-second floor in no time." He tapped the Chevy's roof. "I've got a thirty year old scotch that'll knock your socks off."

Durham smiled. "I'm not wearing socks."

Todd stuck his head in the passenger side and his foggy eyes fell to the floorboard. Hairy ankles. "I'll be damned." He turned to the valet. "Hey, Carlos. My friend's coming up for a minute. Park his car someplace close, would you?"

Carlos nodded and sped off in Todd's BMW.

"Come on." Todd led the way into the grandiose Italian marbled entry that was Port Lauderdale. They had the elevator to themselves until the box stopped at fifteen and two giggling cuties got on with them. Together they might have had forty years between them.

"Evening, ladies," Todd said, with an exaggerated bow.

"Hi," they replied in unison.

"This is my friend, Nicholas."

Durham nodded.

"We're on our way up to my place for a nightcap. Care to join us?"

The door shot open on nineteen and the girls walked out, wiggling their tales behind them. "Sorry," said the taller of the two. Her friend giggled. "We've got dates."

Alone again, Durham said, "Nice try."

"Can't win them all."

Todd was relieved when the elevator stopped on twenty-two. All that drinking was catching up with him. His stomach was getting that queasy feeling again.

"Tell me," said Todd, as Durham helped him get the key in the lock protecting his apartment—the keyhole kept moving, swimming away and the detective helped steady the door, "you ever kill anybody?"

"Nope." Durham pushed open the door and crossed the foyer. He whistled. "Nice view, all right."

Todd grinned with pride. "View of the Intracoastal. Can't beat that."

"I don't even want to know how much this must've cost you."

"You're right, you don't." Todd crossed to the wet bar in the living room. "Let me get you that scotch." He glanced at the phone machine. Thirteen messages. That wasn't lucky. But hell, he'd screen them later.

Durham walked to the window and gazed down at the boats below and the high-rises across the way. "How about you?"

"How about me what?"

"You ever kill anybody?"

Todd set two half-filled glasses on the coffee table. He picked one up and downed its contents. A sudden idea twisted through his brain like a bent paperclip. "No. I haven't."

Durham grabbed his drink and took it out on the balcony. A stiff breeze threw his hair back. Todd thought they guy looked better that way. Less rumpled. More like he actually had made the effort to do something about the way he looked.

"It's a long way down." Durham leaned over the rail. He turned and faced Todd. "You ever worry about falling?"

Todd thought about that a minute. The fact was he felt like he was in freefall now. Between the booze and Doug Freeman the feeling was inevitable. "I'm falling even now."

Durham nodded and leaned back out on the rail, letting the wind carry news of foreign lands. Todd watched. With the sliding doors open, the curtains fluttered like ghosts. He closed his eyes and took a couple of long, slow breaths. He was falling asleep.

Todd forced his eyes open. His glass was slipping from his fingers and he couldn't summon up enough energy to stop the freefall. The detective was looking at him. Todd blinked and his eyes tumbled shut again.

Todd woke with a start. The ghosts were still dancing. The phone was ringing. There was no sign of the detective. Todd groaned as he headed for the phone extension behind the wet bar. An incipient hangover had already begun, and it wasn't even morning. "Hello?"

"Hey there, Todd."

FIVE MINUTES

The hairs on the back of Todd's neck crawled like earthworms. It was Doug.

"I just wanted to thank you for a most pleasant evening. I do hope you and your friend had a good time. How was the chicken? Good?"

The receiver hung in Todd's hand like a five hundred pound anchor.

"Not very talkative tonight, are we, Todd?" Doug chuckled. "I understand. "You must be tired. It has been a long day. I know I'm tired. I'm very tired, Todd," Doug said rather pointedly. "Pleasant dreams."

The click of the phone was like an empty chambered gun going off against Todd's ear. He dropped the receiver and stared at it. It dangled by its cord, twisting in an unseen and impalpable breeze.

Freefall.

That spiraling piece of molded plastic looked more like a replica of himself than a telephone. And the way it hung there, helpless and vulnerable, scared him.

:8

"This is it?" Aristotle Constantine's face was flush and pinched as an angry persimmon. "This is what I paid four fucking million dollars for?"

Todd tugged at his silk tie. Constantine kept the Caddie's air conditioner set at a crisp sixty-five degrees, but the backseat was getting hot anyway. Constantine owned one of those big Escalade ESV's. A black one. Black paint, black leather. The thing was a monster and though Mr. Constantine's flunky, Peter, was along for the ride, Mr. Constantine liked to handle the driving himself. Peter rode shotgun. This was a job that the laconic sidekick seemed built for. Todd had never seen Peter when his spine wasn't as rigid as the barrel of a shotgun.

Todd had the big backseat to himself. The Miami Dolphins could have fit back there with him.

It was a good thing the Escalade's pedals were adjustable because Aristotle Constantine was no bigger than Napoleon on a good day and there'd be no way the little guy could reach the pedals and look out the windshield otherwise. And talk about long. The ESV had to be at least half a block in length. The driver and the rear-most passengers might even be in separate time zones.

"Yes, sir, Mr. Constantine. This is it." Todd's phone had started ringing at seven and it hadn't stopped ringing until Todd finally crawled out of bed and answered it around nine-twenty. That had been Peter, announcing that he and his boss were on their way and would be picking Todd up shortly. "We'll be taking a look at those Boca lots."

Before Todd could refuse or suggest rescheduling, like sometime after his hangover ended in the year 2020, or until Doug called off his fatwah, Peter hung up.

Todd pulled open the fridge and chugged a few ounces of Most Pulp OJ. Most Pulp was right. He coughed and spit bits of pulp, grapefruit pulp no less, into the sink and contemplated breakfast. But his stomach wouldn't hear of it. A flash of white on the dark granite counter caught his eye. He picked it up. So, Detective Nicholas Durham had left his business card.

Todd carried it with him as he went to dress. Durham might come in handy yet.

Now Todd wished he'd had that breakfast. His head was clanging and his belly was screaming. And it didn't help matters or his constitution that Aristotle Constantine's anger was entirely directed at him.

Mr. Constantine was a short, balding Greek who displayed his passion for food and fine living around his middle. He wore a wrinkle-less blue wool suit with a white shirt and matching blue tie. Todd had never seen the man less than elegantly dressed. His assistant, Peter, was a leaner but equally well-dressed version of his master.

"I don't get it," complained Constantine. "Do you get it, Peter?"

"I don't get it, Mr. Constantine." Peter, whom Todd was sure had a last name though he'd never heard it mentioned, was looking at him. His coal gray eyes were saying *What the fuck kind of game are you playing?* and *Do you know how bad I can hurt you?*

"It's not as bad as it looks, I assure you." Todd scooted over to the side nearest the Intracoastal. "You see those markers out there? That's how far your property goes."

"Property!" snorted Constantine.

Todd pressed on. "That big yellow house on the left has about ten feet of setback this way. The rest is yours. Same goes for the other side. You've got yourself the last four developable Intracoastal lots in Boca Raton, Mr. Constantine."

Constantine glared at him. A bit of scrambled egg clung to the Greek's lower lip but Todd didn't dare mention it. "Developable? What am I going to do? Turn this dump into a water-skiing park?"

Peter chuckled. "Good one, Mr. Constantine."

"So, Todd, how much money you think me and my partners are going to make renting water skis to tourists?"

"Mr. Constantine," began Todd, fighting to figure out a way to calm down his best and most dangerous client, "it really isn't as bad as all that. We'll get some earth. Fill it in. You'll see."

"Going to take a lot of dirt."

Todd nodded. A lot of dirt. That was an understatement.

Another fact he didn't dare mention to Constantine, like that egg on his face. But the bottom line was that this was an excellent investment. A guy only had to have vision. Todd had vision. Unfortunately, he didn't have the line of credit to swing a deal this size himself.

Constantine demanded, "How much?"

"How much?" Todd's mind had wandered and he wasn't sure what the old man was talking about.

"How much dirt and how much is it going to cost?"

"I-I'm not sure. I could get you some estimates and—"

Constantine raised his hand. "You do that. And I want the answer in dollars not bullshit. You understand?"

"Yes, sir." The Greek was a pain but a paying one. Todd had a huge commission riding on this deal. If it came unraveled now, his company was going to be out over four hundred grand. "We'll be able to build four big estates here, Mr. Constantine. That house across the street there is about ten thousand feet under air. You'll be able to fit estates that size on each of these four lots."

Todd did some calculating and some exaggerating. "You'll be able to sell them for six to ten million dollars apiece. You and your partners stand to make a nice profit."

Constantine looked out over the swampy landscape. "Houses that big, eh?"

Todd nodded.

"How far you say the lots extend into the Intracoastal?"

"It's hard to say exactly," Todd was riffling through his briefcase, "what with so much of it under water at this time. But according to the papers, the lot line extends from the road here out approximately one hundred twenty-five feet."

Todd looked at the papers. "One hundred twenty-five feet and four inches to be exact. Each lot is a little different in dimensions, but that's about average."

"Hundred and a quarter." Constantine tapped his lips with his index finger and the scrambled egg now clung to the tip of his finger. "Show me."

Todd pushed the papers forward. "You can see here." Todd traced the lots with his fingernail.

"No," said Constantine. "Show me." He looked out the window.

Todd's brow crinkled. "Sir?"

"Out there, Mr. Jones."

"You want me to show you outside?" Todd looked through the tinted windows. It was a freaking swamp out there. You couldn't walk twenty feet without getting your feet wet. What the hell did Constantine expect Todd to show him?

Nonetheless, Todd opened the door and jumped to the ground. He started again to explain the width and breadth of the lots, holding the papers up to his forehead as a visor, protection from the heavy sun overhead.

Tony could see but not hear Constantine speaking with his assistant.

Peter rolled down his window. "Mr. Constantine would like you to walk the lots."

"Walk the—" Todd's mouth stayed open. Normally, such a request was commonplace. He did it all the time with clients.

Peter and Constantine were watching him. Todd walked to the edge of exposed land. Water lapped up to the edges here, as the wake of passing boats reached inland.

"Keep going." Constantine waved Todd on.

Todd bit his tongue. He rolled up his pants, removed his socks and stuffed them into his Cole Haans. He marched forward barefoot. The earth sucked at his toes. The water was warm. He marched on.

The water was up to his knees now. For the first time, Todd wondered if there were alligators or sharks or other fearful denizens of the deep. "My luck, there'll be goddam piranhas," he muttered as he crossed through a patch of half-submerged weeds.

Finally he came to a stop, the water almost to his bellybutton. His suit was ruined. No doubt about that. But it would be worth it if it made Aristotle Constantine happy. A guy could buy a lot of suits for four hundred grand. He stuffed the papers into his inside coat pocket, cupped his hands and shouted, "This looks about right, Mr. Constantine!"

Back in the air-conditioned Caddie, Constantine nodded. "Good. Now maybe you know exactly how much earth is going to be needed to get this lake above water."

Todd watched as Peter's window silently closed. The ESV turned around in the drive across the way. Todd ran, raising his knees high to clear the swamp that was sucking him in. Todd grabbed his shoes and socks, holding them at arm's length to keep from dripping water and muck all over them. The Escalade came around and stopped.

Mr. Constantine rolled down his window. "You get me my dirt."

Constantine finally spotted the scrambled egg on his

finger. He stuck his finger in his mouth and pulled it out with a popping noise. "And be careful, Mr. Jones. These lots look dangerous. A man could get himself killed here and nobody would ever find the corpse."

"Yes, sir, Mr. Constantine. I'll get on that right away. As soon as I get back to my office and—" Todd grabbed the door handle. It was locked.

"You ain't getting in here all gooey like that," said Constantine. "You'll ruin the leather, the carpets."

"But, how—" sputtered Todd.

Constantine hit the gas and the giant Caddie headed south like a mechanized dinosaur in search of better forage.

Todd shook his hands and legs, looking more dog-like than he intended. A foxy young blonde, a typical Boca babe, behind the wheel of a black Mercedes stared at Todd suspiciously as she pulled up to the closed gates of the estate to the north of him.

Todd thought about going over and introducing himself as her new neighbor, but the Boca bitch just might have a diamond and jewel encrusted gun.

Probably shoot gold bullets, too.

:9

The yellow Porsche came out of nowhere. Fast.

Todd swiveled, looking for shelter, someplace to hide. But there was nothing, except the estates across the street and on each side of the empty lots. Not good options. If he tried to scale any of those high walls, he'd probably get shot as a hostile intruder. Assuming he made it past the ubiquitous guard dogs; Doberman pinschers with a craving for human flesh.

The car was a good hundred yards away. There was only one clear choice.

Todd headed toward deep water. He splashed through the swampy lots past the spot he'd stopped for that crazy Constantine and dove. As Todd performed a gangly swan dive, he twisted his neck. If he was going to get plugged, he wanted to see his killer.

As he hit the water, his only thoughts were *Shit, it's a goddamn Boxster.*

Todd surfaced and climbed to his knees. The water had been more shallow than he'd been expecting. And rocky.

He'd bruised his ribs on some submerged coral or something. Todd brushed wet hair out of his face.

The Porsche had come to a stop at the Tuscan villa across the street. Looked like someplace Mussolini might have lived out his retirement years in had he got that chance. *Shit, not only was it a Boxster, it was a freaking convertible.* Why hadn't he recognized this before diving in?

Todd cursed himself. He slammed a fist against the surface of the causeway and was rewarded with an eyeful of stinging salt water. His scream carried over the water.

The driver was looking at him. A young man in surfer duds with bleached blond hair. One of those kids who probably didn't have to lift a finger in life, thought Todd with no little amount of jealousy. His own life had never been so easy.

And it seemed to be getting harder by the minute. What had he done to deserve this? he wondered.

The kid sauntered over, watching Todd as he scrambled back up to dry land, with his hands stuffed in his baggy red shorts and finally said, "What's up, dude? You okay?"

Todd tossed his left shoe and sock on the ground near surfer boy's feet. His other shoe had drifted out into deep water and Todd had been afraid to follow after it. The effort would probably have proven useless, anyway. The shoe would sink before he could reach it, or he'd just get run over by some speedboat, one of those grotesque-looking cigarette boats. Todd could see his two hundred dollar Cole Haan cruising past the channel marker now, his sock a makeshift sail.

That was the sort of luck he seemed to be having.

"What the hell have I done to deserve this?"

"What, bro'?"

Todd looked up. He'd forgotten the kid was there. "Nothing. Talking to myself."

The young man nodded as if this was a perfectly ordinary thing for a guy in a soaking wet, fifteen hundred dollar Hugo Boss suit to be doing.

Todd sniffed, filling his nostrils with saltwater. Tears welled up in the corners of his still tender eyes. "Have you got a phone I can use to call my office?"

Not only should he be checking in with the office, he should be checking in with Holly. He hadn't spoken to his girlfriend since this whole crazy thing with Doug had started.

What if Doug had told Holly about his fooling around with Caroline? Half the messages on his machine at home had probably been from her. Would they be friendly, concerned messages or was he in trouble deep? The answer would have to wait. With Constantine hauling him out of his condo first thing in the morning, Todd hadn't had time to listen to his phone messages.

If Holly was going to find out he'd cheated on her, it was best coming from him not Deranged Doug.

"Sure." The kid whipped a shiny, silver cellphone from his shorts. It was one of those fancy ones that took digital photographs.

Why was Todd not surprised? Maybe he'd get this kid to snap his picture. One of those 'before and after' deals. The scary thing was, if this was 'before', what was 'after' going to look like?

Todd dialed. There was no answer except for the

recorded voice of his receptionist saying that the office was closed for the afternoon. He returned the phone.

"No luck?"

Todd shook his head. "What day is this?"

"Saturday, dude."

Todd rubbed his face. Hard. Any harder and his nose would have rubbed off in his hands. He'd promised everybody who didn't have scheduled appointments the day off. He was also supposed to have breakfast with Holly.

He looked at his damp watch.

Two and one-quarter hours ago.

"Anybody else you want to call?"

Todd considered. He could call Holly. But what would he tell her? She was bound to ask questions. Just look at him. Who wouldn't have questions? "No. A cab, maybe."

"Where you want to go?"

"How about the Bahamas?"

The kid held out his hand. "I'm Steve." He jerked his thumb toward the car. "I've got wheels. I'll give you a lift."

"Todd. Todd Jones." They shook. Todd noticed that Steve had a solitary, dime-sized, 18kt gold loop earring in his right ear. Todd had thought about getting an earring once. It had been Holly's idea. Todd told her it was bad for business. He had an image to maintain, after all.

Todd quickly assessed the stranger. All in all, the kid looked normal enough. Why not let Steve give him a lift? Make his own life easier. Todd said, "You sure?"

"I'm sure. I'm not doing anything."

That much Todd believed.

"Some place short of the Bahamas, that is." Steve

grinned. "I don't have enough gas in the tank for that trip, bro'. "

Todd thanked Steve and they walked, rather Steve walked and Todd squished, their way to the Boxster. "I'm afraid I'll get your car all wet."

Steve shrugged. "Not to worry. I've got a blanket in the trunk." True to his word, Steve pulled a blue and green beach blanket from the front trunk and Todd spread it over the passenger seat.

"What were you doing out there, anyway?"

Todd forced a smile. "Showing some property." The air was beginning to dry him out. Nothing like a convertible on a sun-filled Florida day to put you through the dry cycle.

Steve shot him an amused look. "Dude, you realtors are really wacked, aren't you?"

Todd ran his fingers through his almost dry hair. "I'm not as crazy as I must have looked to you, Steve. I don't normally go jumping into the Intracoastal in my business suit."

Steve's guffaw cut through the sound of the breeze and the thrum of the engine. "That was hilarious, dude. The way you went running out into the Intracoastal like that as I was coming up the street. I thought I was having flashbacks or hallucinations or something."

"I aim to please."

"No offense. My old man says real estate salesmen are jerks. Again, no offense."

"None taken." Todd closed his eyes and raised his face to the sun. May as well work on his tan while he was here. "What does your old man do?"

"Manufactures guns."

"Manufactures guns?" And the man called realtors jerks?

"That's right."

"Like in Bang! Bang! You're dead?"

"Yeah, dude. Small arms, rifles, some custom stuff. You name it, Dad's got it."

"Me, I'm not into guns. Hate 'em," said Steve. "But Dad makes me keep a couple in the car for protection. You know." To prove his point, Steve yanked a big, ugly black revolver of some kind from under his seat and waved it in Todd's face. "See?"

Todd backed away. His eyes bulged. "Yeah, I see." He pushed against the door. End of the line. "Steve, put that thing away."

Steve shrugged and stuffed it under his seat. "There's one under your seat, too."

Todd squirmed, feeling much like the princess in the Princess and the Pea story. He would swear he could feel that gun under his butt. It was impossible, of course, but he'd swear it anyway. "Are those things loaded?"

"Of course, they're loaded. What the hell good is an empty gun? You don't want to aim a gun at somebody unless you're prepared to pull the trigger and blow him," pronounced Steve, "or her, away. Dad always says that."

Fatherly words of wisdom from some fractured universe, mused Todd. A universe he was hoping to steer this spaceship away from.

To this end, Todd looked anxiously around for someplace practical for Surfer Steve to drop him off.

:10

Steve didn't give him the chance.

Todd held on as Steve sped up Dixie Highway, cut across the train tracks just before the gates came down for the freight train heading their way and spun into the driveway of a flat-roofed, shoebox-sized house a block from the tracks. Steve parked behind a red Pontiac Firebird, circa 1990, in cherry condition.

The house seemed to shake as the freight train, loaded with gravel, passed. Paint peeled from the walls of the house as if it was so old it couldn't bear to hold on any longer. All the windows and the front door, a beat up swatch of pink, were barred.

Looking around, Todd noticed that all the houses on the narrow street were barred. And every yard he could see into had a chainlink fence around the back. Behind this house's fence, Todd spotted a hungry looking Rottweiler who was currently using a couple of steel links for dental floss.

The whole area looked more like a minimum security prison than a neighborhood. Not exactly the investment type property that Todd was used to. What the hell was Steve doing here? What was *he* doing here? "What the hell are we doing?"

Steve cut the engine. "Since we're in the neighborhood, I thought I'd make a quick pickup. Don't worry, I'll get something for you, too, 'bro."

Todd blanched. Was Psycho Steve talking about drugs? A wave of paranoia washed over him. "That's okay. I don't need anything. Except to get home and get out of these filthy clothes."

Todd's breath was coming out in shallow pulls. A motley crew of youths hovered over an aging forest green Buick 225 parked across the street, eying them warily. It seemed to Todd that they were hungrily eying the Porsche as well.

This was not good. This was not a good place to be.

Steve pulled that ugly black revolver from under the driver's seat and stuffed it into his shirt. "No trouble. Good stuff. You'll see. And you'll be home in no time."

Steve rapped his knuckles on the door panel. "Be right back."

Todd scrunched down in his seat. Through the sideview mirror he could see those kids looking at him. Was he on their menu?

Several uneasy minutes passed. Todd kept his eyes on the house. The corner of one of the beige curtains flapped up, then fell.

Todd heard shots. "What the—"

The front door flew open. Steve, a stupid smile plastered all over his face, was running for the car. He had a paper bag in one hand and that ugly black gun in the other. "Shoot the bastards, Todd. Shoot 'em!"

Steve dodged between the Firebird and the Boxster. Moving only on reflex and instinct to survive, Todd reached under his seat, felt cold metal, and pulled. Somehow, a gun was in his hand. He closed his eyes and started firing. Chunks of cement block went flying. There was the sound of broken glass. He heard screams.

The revolver bucked in his trembling hand as he fired wildly. Todd could no longer hold on to the weapon. It fell inside his coat. He could feel the hot barrel burning a hole in his side.

The kids across the street had scattered.

Steve burned rubber, backing up, jumping the curb, and peeling down the street.

They surged down the road parallel to the train tracks and lost themselves in traffic.

Todd's heart was pounding in his throat. "What was that all about?"

Steve still had that stupid grin on his face. "Alvin looked out the window and saw you sitting out in my car. The guys don't like surprises."

Neither do I, thought Todd. "Do you think they'll follow us?" He looked back anxiously.

"Nah. They were only trying to make a point."

Todd shivered. Their point was well taken.

The Port Lauderdale Condominium Towers never looked so good to Todd. He felt like he'd been gone a lifetime. In the last couple of days, Todd always felt like he'd already used up a couple of lives as well.

Todd set his shaky legs on the pavement. "Thanks for the

lift." The front end of Steve's Boxster bore several fresh bullet holes. He told Steve.

"No biggie," said Steve, his hands draped over the wheel. "I'll drop the car off at the dealer's. They'll fix it up again."

Again? wondered Todd. How often was Steve shot at by his drug dealer? Sounded like Alvin and Steve had one interesting relationship. And Todd thought he had interpersonal relationship issues.

Steve reached into the paper sack he'd brought out of the house in Pompano. He threw a small baggy at Todd. Todd caught it in his hand. It was pot. "Told you I'd get you a little something."

Todd hid the little bag under his wrinkled coat. The doorman was helping a resident into a taxi. What if he'd been seen with drugs? "I don't think I should—"

Steve put the Boxster in gear and pulled away. "Hang in there, Todd!"

Todd's shoulders collapsed as Steve literally left him holding the bag. He turned to go into the building and felt something hard bumping against his ribs.

The revolver!

Todd ran out to the center of the circle. Steve was rounding the side, slowed by the taxi. "Hey, Steve!"

Steve braked.

"You forgot your—" Todd glanced over his shoulder. The day doorman was leaning over his stand, looking their way. Todd mouthed, "Gun."

Steve looked puzzled.

Todd mouthed again. "G-U-N. Gun."

"Oh. I got plenty of the things. You keep it. A souvenir."

"But I don't want—"

Steve waved and, with a roar that cut out Todd's pleas, the Boxster zoomed off.

Todd stood in the center of the drive, wanting nothing more than to collapse right there. Maybe melt into the ground and be reincarnated as something more simple, carefree, like a Monarch butterfly. Big yellow and orange wings carrying him from chrysanthemum to sunflower to daffodil.

But he couldn't collapse now. He had a bag full of pot in his pants and a recently fired gun in his shirt.

Todd turned and marched to the foyer, holding his coat close to his chest. He had a morbid fear that the gun was going to fall or that the doorman was somehow going to see it with his x-ray vision or something.

But Todd, despite his fears, made it to the elevator safely. And there was no sign of Doug. Too bad. It might have been a relief if Doug had just popped out from behind a potted plant and put a nice cold bullet between his eyes.

Todd hit the button and soared. Doug was trying to kill him. Aristotle Constantine was threatening to kill him and now a bunch of whacked out drug dealers led by some maniac named Alvin might be after him as well.

What else could go wrong?

Todd dangled his keychain looking for the house key. He gave a start as the knob turned and the door opened without his assistance. "Holly!"

:11

Holly's mouth hung open wide enough for a 747 to squeeze through and still have room for a flock of geese heading the other way.

Todd stammered, "Wh-what are you doing here?"

More importantly: how was he going to get rid of her? He had drugs and a gun. Doug was trying to murder him and Constantine wanted his stinking dirt. Alvin and his Drugmunks were probably carrying a grudge for him and Steve shooting up their crack house.

What if those crazy dealers found out where he lived?

And what if Doug came and hurt him and Holly both? Or worse, what if Doug told Holly about Caroline? Lord, he'd really be in trouble then!

Holly's left heel tapped out an indecipherable code against the imported limestone floor. She wore a sexy, tight-fitting, black jumpsuit with a deep-V front and beaded neckline. The small beads, as irregular as baby peas, were lavender and set off her clair de lune eyes, very pale blue with a tinge of lavender. Holly's eyes reminded Todd of Chinese porcelain.

And like porcelain, Holly's eyes could be delicate, yet so hard.

Her tapping feet were swaddled in black patent leather, retro-style Forties pumps with open sides and mary jane straps and peek-a-boo toes. "I was looking for you." Her nose wrinkled up. Her eyes fell to his bare feet. "What happened to you?"

Todd tugged at his damp jacket. The gun was chafing his rib cage. "I was showing a client some property."

Her Barbie doll eyes were the size of espresso saucers. "What client?" Her usually liquid and sensual voice was a few notches tighter and squeakier than usual.

"Ari. Aristotle Constantine." He pushed inside. It was his apartment after all.

"Oh."

That seemed to satisfy her. Constantine's reputation preceded him. They guy also had a twenty-million dollar line of credit at Florida Sunshine Savings and Loan. Holly had told Todd about it. In fact, she was responsible for connecting Todd up with Mr. Constantine.

"Want a drink?"

"I was hoping we could go to lunch," said Holly, crossing her arms. "I haven't had any breakfast."

Ouch. A straight thrust right to the gut. "Sorry. Constantine called from right outside the building and practically dragged me out of bed. I didn't have much choice. You know how he is."

Holly nodded. She knew very well. He was a determined businessman. And a determined ladies' man.

Todd went to the bar and poured himself a generous and much deserved glass of Bushmill's Malt. Aged twenty-one years in madeira drums, the single malt Irish whiskey was about a hundred bucks a bottle and Todd figured he'd just swilled about seven or eight dollar's worth.

The drink had solved his immediate problems. Now what was he going to do about Holly?

Holly sighed. "Why don't you get cleaned up? I'll fix us something."

Todd smiled. "That'd be great. Hey, we can eat out on the patio."

He listened to the domestic sounds of Holly in the kitchen. Refrigerator and cabinets opening and closing. Tinkling silverware. "How did you get in the apartment anyway?"

"The doorman let me in," she called out.

Todd nodded. He was going to have to do something about that. He quietly dialed downstairs and left instructions that no one was ever again to be allowed up without his express permission. That included Mr. Constantine, Thug Peter, and any drug salesmen.

Damn, he should have specifically included Surfer Steve as well. Oh well. He'd deal with that later.

Holly was still talking. "I was so worried about you. You never called me back last night and then you didn't show up this morning."

"I had a client last night. We had dinner."

"Where?"

"Paddy's."

"Oh. Sell anything?"

Todd thought about Det. Durham. "Not yet, but if I'm lucky, something will come of it."

If he could only figure out a way for Det. Durham to kill Doug for him, everything would be hunky-dory once more.

"By the way, Doug called."

Todd dropped his glass. Had she reached in and snatched one of his thoughts right out of his head? Was she clairvoyant? The glass rattled around his feet. Good thing it was empty. "What?"

Holly stuck her head around the corner. "I said Doug called."

Todd fought to compose himself. "When? Where?"

Holly shrugged. "A little while ago."

"What did he say?"

"Not much. Only that he wants you to call him."

Fat chance, thought Todd.

"He's been acting weird lately," said Holly, tossing some tomatoes into an avocado salad.

"Weird? Weird how?"

"I don't know exactly. But when I talked to him yesterday—"

Todd hurried to the kitchen and pulled Holly around.

"Hey, careful! You almost made me drop the bowl, silly."

"Sorry." He forced himself to appear calm. "You spoke to Doug yesterday?"

"Uh-huh. When you didn't call me last night, I got worried. I remembered you were having your physical with Doug and I thought maybe you'd had some bad news. So I phoned him."

"What did he say?"

"Nothing. I asked him where you were. He said you left his office around six and that was the last he'd seen of you. But when I asked him about your checkup, if you were okay, he said it was too soon to tell. That seemed kind of funny to me."

Yeah, thought Todd, Doug was probably waiting for the coroner's report after Todd's body was discovered riddled with bullets.

Todd performed a mental impersonation of his nemesis: *I won't lie to you. I'm afraid it doesn't look like Todd's going to pull through, Holly.*

"Are you okay, Todd?"

"Sure. Fit as the proverbial fiddle." Todd slapped his chest. "I don't know why Doug didn't tell you so. Doctor-patient confidentiality, I guess."

"You should call him." Holly pulled free and carried the salad plates to the balcony.

"I will," said Todd, "right after I shower."

"Please do," replied Holly, wrinkling her nose again. "That reminds me," she said, "who's Det. Durham?"

"Detective Durham?" Todd spoke as if his words were skating on thin ice.

"Yes. He came by a little while ago."

"Here?"

Holly nodded. "He'd left his sunglasses behind."

"Oh, Nicholas Durham. He's the client I was with last night. I forgot he was detective."

"Anyway, I gave him my card. I explained to him that Florida Sunshine loves working with law enforcement. I can get him a great rate right now."

"I didn't even know he was looking." Oops. Todd realized his faux pas.

"Huh?"

"I mean for a mortgage already. I guess he really is serious about buying something." Sometimes Todd scared himself, he was that good. "Anything else to tell me?" Like Doug Freeman was hiding in the bedroom closet waiting to kill him, maybe?

"No, that's it. Go get bathed. I'll finish setting up lunch."

Todd pecked Holly's soft, warm cheek. "Right."

She sniffed and waved her hand in front of her perfect nose. "And wash your hair. You smell like you've been swimming in the sewer or something."

"Yes, dear." He padded towards the master bath.

"And hurry," Holly commanded from the kitchen stove. "I'm starting the omelet. Besides, you don't want to be all smelly when Doug gets here."

Todd stopped in his tracks. "Doug?"

"Yes, he said he might stop by sometime this afternoon."

Todd nodded glumly. It was going to be a long day.

If he lived.

:12

The shower did him no good. He came out sweating bullets. Soon-to-be real ones.

But there was no budging Holly. Not unless he wanted to come clean with her. Which he did not.

After what had seemed to him an interminable lunch, Todd managed to get rid of Holly by pleading that he had work to do for Mr. Constantine. He promised her dinner at the restaurant of her choosing to make up for his bad behavior.

She allowed Todd to fawn awhile and finally picked a Mexican place in Coconut Grove, a hip little town on the southwestern outskirts of Miami. At first, Todd wasn't thrilled with the thought of driving all the way down to Miami, but the more he thought about it, the more he liked the idea.

Doug's job of finding him would be a lot more difficult if Todd was in Miami.

Todd stuffed the bag of pot, along with the deadly firearm, under his mattress, a time-honored tradition, and rang for his car. It was waiting for him when he hit the lobby.

A quick scan told him Doug was nowhere around, at least not that Todd could see.

What Todd needed was a plan. Not more of this flying by the seat of his pants garbage. One hand on the wheel, he retrieved his wallet from his chinos. It was still damp. Maybe ruined. Todd cursed. Goddamn alligator hide ought to be waterproof, oughtn't it? Alligators spend their lives in the freaking water.

He pulled Det. Durham's business card from the billfold. Soaked through and falling apart, Todd could make out Det. Durham's name okay, but the address was tougher. He'd have to wing it.

The car phone started singing as he turned onto Sunrise Boulevard, a major roadway running east to west, following the sun. Durham lived out in Plantation. Westward, Ho!

"Yeah? Todd Jones here." Todd turned down the CD player.

"Good morning, Todd."

Todd's lips turned sharply downward. It was Doug Freeman. He looked in his rearview mirror. Was that a yellow car back there behind that Expedition in the next lane? "It's afternoon."

"My mistake." Doug's breathing was heavy. "Trusting you was another."

"Look, Doug," said Todd, "I am really and truly sorry. I know I did a really lousy thing."

"You fucked my wife."

"I made a mistake. Can't we put all this behind us?"

There was a long silence filled only with the sounds of

traffic. Todd pressed the phone closer to his ear. He could discern traffic sounds coming from the other end, too. That meant Doug was in his car. Todd scanned the road.

Nothing.

"Sure, Todd," said Doug with a voice that sounded all sweet on the surface and all too deadly beneath. "We can put this all behind us—just as soon as I've killed you and said the eulogy at your funeral."

Todd was tempted to tell Doug that he'd have to catch him first, but there seemed no point in goading the guy on.

"You don't want to do that," said Todd. Stopped for a red light at the intersection of Sunrise and 441, he slouched down in his seat, lest Doug was getting ready to take aim from somewhere—like maybe from behind the dumpster tucked up against the back wall of that mini-mart over there. "Think what it will do to your practice, to your wife. You'll be ruined."

"The police would have to catch me for that to happen. And they won't."

"Are you so sure of that?"

Doug laughed. "Positive."

"Seems like the kind of dumb attitude that gets criminals caught every day, Doug. Give it up. Go home and enjoy the rest of your weekend. By Monday, I'll bet you'll see how silly you're behaving."

"You think I'm silly and dumb, Todd?" There was a brittle, cold and frightening coating to Doug's voice. Todd thought that Doug sounded a lot like Hal, that unfeeling, amoral and, face it, psycho computer in Arthur C. Clarke's 2001, A Space Odyssey.

"Uh, no," replied Todd quickly. "I didn't mean that exactly." Jesus, now the nutjob was going to get all sensitive on him.

"Because I'm not silly and dumb."

"I know you're not, buddy."

"For instance, I could kill you right now, blow your fucking head off, but there are too many people around. And all stuck in traffic."

The damn traffic signal still hadn't changed to green.

"Not good. I might get caught."

Todd forced a chuckle. "Right. You're probably a hundred miles away." Nonetheless, Todd scrunched down even lower in his seat.

"Really? You mean you aren't waiting for the light to change driving your Beemer, headed west on Sunrise Boulevard at the intersection of State Road 441?"

Shit. Todd's heart revved. If there hadn't been a car in front of him blocking the way, he'd have made a dash through oncoming traffic. At least he had a chance of surviving that. And the Beemer did have an airbag system. What it didn't have was a bulletproof driver's vest.

Doug was laughing. "Look behind you."

Todd stuck his head between the front seats and took a peek. A creamy white Lexus was directly behind. The driver, wearing a ballcap, waved.

"Bang, bang, you're dead. It's a rental, Todd. So now who's silly and dumb?"

Todd's foot hit the accelerator. To tell the truth, he wasn't sure if he meant to or his foot slipped. No matter. He bumped into the red Chrysler 300 in front of him. Both cars rocked. When the shake, rattle and rolling subsided, a bruiser and his wife piled out of the Chrysler.

Meanwhile, the traffic light had changed to green and Doug sped around and away.

Sonofabitch.

"Where the hell did you learn to drive?" shouted the bruiser's wife, with a voice like a bent and out-of-tune, low-end trumpet, while the bruiser himself, a ruddy faced, brown-headed fellow with a belly that protruded past his expansive pecs, folded his arms and displayed his biceps.

After exchanging phone numbers and insurance information with the bruiser in the Chrysler and his fuming wife, Todd continued on his journey. The more he looked at the detective's business card, the clearer the print became. He'd deciphered the street and had the number down to a digit or two.

That was close enough, because Durham was in his front yard, as if expecting him. This was just too easy.

The Durham residence was a fairly average home for the neighborhood and, except for the differences in trim color, red versus blue versus green, one house seemed pretty much indistinguishable from any other. Todd guessed this was a four bedroom, two bath box with about eighteen hundred feet under air.

Det. Durham, in an extra-large Miami Dolphins shirt and a pair of khaki shorts was out front pushing a lawnmower around on the grass. Clippings flew around his white-socked ankles like angry green insects. Neighbors on each side were doing pretty much the same thing—clipping, cutting, edging.

Both the nearest neighbors stopped to look for a moment

as Todd parked the silver BMW on the street in front of Durham's house. The detective himself kept on cutting. Never looking up.

Todd leaned on his horn. That got Nicholas Durham's attention. He killed the power to the mower and wiped his damp brow with the back of his dirty mitt.

The instant the engine died, the front door flew open and a witch—there was no other way Todd felt he could justly describe her—stuck her head out. Her long nose stuck forward like a coat hook. Her skin was so white it looked like she'd spent her life underground like one of those naked mole rats.

"What'd you stop for, Nicky?" Her red hair, full of big pink curlers, shook. "I told you you need to finish before my mom gets here."

Durham rolled his eyes for only Todd to see. "I've got company," he said, without looking at his wife. "Give it a rest, will you?"

His answer came in the form of a slammed door.

The detective grabbed the bag off the lawn mower and dumped the shavings into a green trash barrel. "That was Trish."

Todd nodded. Silent communication seemed to pass between them. A guy thing.

Maybe it was the realtor in him, but Todd always believed that seeing where a man lived increased one's understanding of the man. That seemed apparent in Det. Durham's case. It was no wonder the detective hadn't been in a hurry to get home the other night.

"Welcome to my humble abode." Durham let the grass

catcher fall to the ground and gave it a kick.

Todd nodded. "Nice place."

"Rii-ight," the detective drawled.

Todd noticed Durham's neighbors had gone back to their own yard work. Probably scared of their own wives. Who knew? Maybe the whole neighborhood was home to a coven of witches.

"So," Durham looked Todd in the eye, "what brings you here?"

"Thought I'd make sure you got home all right."

"I did." Durham glanced back at his house. "You want a beer?"

"Sure."

"Come on." Durham crossed the lawn to his neighbor's house. The neighbor, a rail of a man with red beard was savagely attacking the hedge that formed a dividing line between the two yards.

The red bearded man one-handedly waved his clippers.

"That's Alan." Durham walked into the neighbor's garage where there was an old green side-by-side refrigerator tucked into the back corner beside some dust-shrouded Titleist golf clubs. Todd hadn't seen a green refrigerator since the Middle Ages, not counting that time he left the Gruyere in the back of his fridge for thirteen months behind the unopened jar of jalapeno jelly that Holly had given him as a gift for his birthday.

"Your neighbor, Alan, doesn't mind that you help yourself to his beer?"

Doug opened his Budweiser and drank before replying. "It's my beer. The wife doesn't like me drinking, so Alan lets me keep my stash here."

Todd grinned.

"I met your girlfriend." Doug leaned against Alan's workbench.

"So I heard."

"You were right."

"About what?"

"About how good looking she is."

"I told you."

Durham tossed his empty bottle in a blue recycle bin where it clattered against its mates. "You could've been bullshitting."

Todd shrugged. "Your wife is pretty good looking, too." Hey, what else could he say?

Durham laughed aloud. He was staring out his neighbor's garage. "Say, there's another yellow Porsche like last night. Don't see many of those in this neighborhood."

Durham spat into the grass. "Hell, I've never seen one in this neighborhood. The guy must be lost." The detective turned to Todd. "You seem to attract them like a magnet."

Todd stuck his head around the corner as the Porsche passed. Had that been Doug? Had he ditched the rental and gone back to his own car?

"Nice set of wheels." Durham sighed. "Not that there's anything wrong with that BMW you drive. Except for that dent in the front." He crossed the lawn and inspected the front end of Todd's 540i. "Don't remember seeing that yesterday. What happened?"

Todd shrugged it off. "A little fender-bender. It was nothing." His palms were sweaty. He wiped them on his pants, leaving dark, uneven streaks. "You said a guy was driving that Porsche?"

"That's right."

"It'd be funny if it was the same driver we saw last night, wouldn't it?" Todd curved his lips into a large, forced smile that he hoped didn't look too disingenuous. "It wasn't, was it?"

Durham seemed to be looked at Todd funny. "Hard to tell. The man was wearing a hat."

A hat? Doug was wearing a ballcap. "What, something like one of those Tampa Bay ball caps?"

"Could've been." Durham peered through the window of Todd's car. "To tell you the truth, I was paying a whole hell of a lot more attention to the car than its driver."

"Sure." Todd watched the detective nervously, wondering what he was looking for.

Durham glanced back at the house with something approaching fear and loathing. "I really should finish up the lawn."

"Of course," said Todd, standing there awkwardly a moment, unsure how to begin to broach the subject foremost on his mind. Did Det. Durham really think Todd had driven all the way out to Plantation on a Saturday to see how he was doing? The smell of fresh grass tickled his nose. He felt a sneeze fit coming on.

A teenage girl in indigo short-shorts and a flamingo pink bikini top stood in the driveway across the street washing a red Volkswagen Jetta. A girl like that could get a man in trouble.

As if reading Todd's mind, Durham said, "Celia's only

seventeen."

Todd reddened.

"She's a good kid. But give her time, I'm sure she'll make some man a great ex-wife."

The detective's words were laden with bitterness. Todd was right about this guy, he just knew it. "You ever thought about doing something different with your life?"

Durham chewed his lip. "Like what?"

"Real estate maybe?"

The detective laughed. "I don't think so. Fifteen more years and I'm eligible for a decent pension. Why would I want to change jobs now?"

Todd watched as the girl across the street leaned over and picked up a washrag. She leaned over the roof of the Volkswagen and scrubbed. A ball of soap foam no larger than a marshmallow clung to her breastplate before she offhandedly wiped it away. Todd said, "No offense, but you don't seem all that happy."

Durham seemed to find this amusing. "There's all sorts of ways to be unhappy." He folded his arms, his gaze mimicking Todd's. "But I love my job. Could use a little extra money, though."

The statement seemed to float before Todd's nose like a potentially record-setting tarpon—Todd had visions of a two hundred pounder, seven foot long—waiting to be hooked. "Maybe I can help you there."

Durham's eyes twinkled. "You mean you didn't drive thirty miles out my way to see if I got home okay, buddy?"

Todd shook his head, ever so slowly.

:13

Even though he and Holly were only going to the Grove, Todd dressed up. South Florida chic. Sports coat, slacks, dress shirt and brown Mephistos.

Holly was dressed to severely disable if not kill outright. Her clingy purple dress and matching pointy shoes said 'look at me.' The figure the dress was wrapped around said 'keep on looking.'

Todd enjoyed the fleshly view. And he did his best to lavish attention on Holly every minute of the drive. Coconut Grove was bustling. Another Saturday night in the neighborhood where it was all about seeing and being seen. They dropped the BMW at the valet's stand across from Senor Frog's and found a table out-of-doors.

Todd would have preferred inside where it was a bit cooler, but Holly wanted to sit outside and watch the parade of see and be seen scenesters go by. Todd wasn't inclined to argue. He'd be exposed, but Doug would never find him here. The guy wasn't superhuman after all.

He could relax for a change. With that in mind, Todd

ordered them each strawberry margaritas.

"I had a call from Mr. Constantine this afternoon."

"He called you at home?"

Holly nodded.

"Couldn't he wait until Monday?"

"I don't mind. He said he wanted to start a spec house on one of the four lots you've sold him and wondered if I could get him a preferred rate."

"What'd you tell him?"

"I told him yes, of course. What else could I tell him?"

Todd shrugged and bit into his enchilada. The spices made his eyes water and he sniffled. He'd ordered the chicken enchiladas and Holly had ordered up the shrimp fajitas—the most expensive item on the menu. Holly didn't come cheap. And it wasn't that Todd didn't think she was worth it, if only she'd eat some of what she ordered.

Holly liked to scoot her food around on a plate, like she was playing a solitary game of checkers. Every once in a while, a bite accidently made it into her mouth and she puckered up and chewed and swallowed. But that wasn't often.

Todd figured he shouldn't complain. How would Holly look if she ate all the food she'd ever ordered? There would be much more of her, that was for certain. But was that a good thing?

"Are you going to get him his dirt?"

"I'm looking into it." Todd ordered a second margarita. Or was it his third? "Look, do we have to talk business? I've had about all I can stand today of Constantine and real estate and I've especially had enough conversation about dirt."

Todd wiped his face with his napkin.

"Sorry."

Todd sighed. He'd been trying to be nice and instead he'd snapped. "I'm sorry, too. Let's just forget all our troubles and have some fun. After dinner, we'll hit one of the nightclubs over here or cruise on over to South Beach." He wiggled in his chair, hands high. "Do a little cha-cha-cha."

Holly leaned forward and planted a kiss on his cheek. "That sounds—"

"Doug!" Acting on instinct, Todd thrust out his hand and pushed Holly's forehead back and over. Her chin bounced off the tabletop. "Get down!" Todd half-rose and shoved Holly under the table. Her shoulder scraped the side and she cried out. Salsa sailed.

Too late! Todd froze. Holly was under the table on her knees. Senor Frog patrons were looking around like there was going to be a stage show.

Doug walked up, opened up his coat and drew out a black, long -barreled pistol. Slowly, Doug's arm came up and he fired.

Todd watched, unable to move or cry out. It was all happening in slow motion, just like in the movies. Something hit him in the face, above the bridge of his nose. He blinked, felt something liquid and wet.

Blood?

Doug was grinning. He waved the pistol in the air and marched on up the sidewalk towards the center of the Grove.

Todd's heart beat with the speed of hummingbirds' wings. But he was still breathing, he noted, still seeing. What the?

He put his hand to his face and examined the liquid. Water. It was only water.

Holly climbed out from under the table. Her knees were black with dirt and bits of food, mostly nacho crumbs. Her shoulder was scraped raw. Her dress and shoes were a mess of guacamole, salsa and strawberry margarita. She brushed herself off and dropped down in her chair. "Are you crazy, Todd? What was that all about?"

Their server, in the company of the manager, came over to see if everything was all right. Todd insisted everything was fine. The server handed Holly a damp towel to wipe herself up with.

"That was Doug." Fucking water. Goddamn Doug had shot him with a water pistol.

"I know it was Doug. I'm not an idiot. I saw him. What on earth did you push me under the table for? You trying to kill me?"

Todd, who'd been watching the street, suddenly turned to her. "No, of course not. It's Doug who's—"

"It's Doug who's what?" Holly was futilely dabbing at her dress with the wet cleaning rag.

Todd frowned. No, he couldn't tell her that Doug was trying to murder him. She'd only want to know why. He shook his head. A goddamn water pistol. What did Doug think he was doing? What was the point of—

And then Todd realized. It was a joke.

Doug was showing Todd just how easy it would be to kill him. Anytime, anyplace.

Todd shivered and righted his listing margarita glass. He drained what dribble remained.

"What on earth was Doug doing shooting you with a watergun?"

Todd shrugged. "A prank, I guess."

"A prank!" Holly's voice shot above the din of the restaurant. She shook her head. "Men can be so juvenile. And just look what you've done to my outfit."

"Sorry." Todd tried to help scrape a pool of salsa from the depression in her shoulder but she pushed him off. "I wonder how he even knew we were here. I mean, I can't believe he happened to be strolling the Grove with a squirtgun and decided to blast us."

"That part, at least, is easy. I told him."

"You?" What was she thinking? thought Todd. Didn't she realize how dumb and dangerous that was? No, he realized, she didn't.

"That's right. He called me at home. Said he wanted to see me, to talk, soon, alone. But I told him I couldn't, not tonight, because we were having dinner here in the Grove. Sounded pretty mysterious to me."

Todd was nodding. "That's odd, all right." And Doug knew that Frog's was one of their favorite restaurants in the Grove.

"Yes, it is. What's got into Doug, anyway?" She glared accusingly at Todd. "Did you do something to make him mad?"

"No, of course not. Not that I know of."

"What about Caroline?"

Todd's radar went on full alert. Did Holly know? Was this D-Day? D-Night?

"Yes. Is Doug having problems with Caroline?"

82

"Not that he mentioned." Todd grinned inwardly. A plan bubbled to the surface. Holly had given him an idea. "Though you may be right. Doug might be hurting. Maybe," said Todd, "this is all a cry for help. He could be walking the street right now, begging, no, praying," Todd corrected, laying it on thick, "that I'll run after him and give him a sympathetic ear."

Todd rose before Holly could figure out what he was up to or raise an objection. He kissed Holly on the cheek. It tasted like guacamole and CoverGirl makeup. "Thanks, Holly. Order us some more drinks. I'll be back soon."

Todd dodged between tables and ran off into the darkness. Holly's words of startled protested barely registered.

Todd walked quickly up the busy sidewalk toward the center of Coconut Grove, following the crowd, jostling the slow walkers in his haste. He kept his eyes peeled. He couldn't afford to let Doug catch him by surprise again. Doug might shoot him with a real gun the next time.

It was dark. Every body was a shadow until it fell under the lights of a street lamp or the glare of a car or the splash of color coming from a storefront.

Todd stopped at every corner, looking in every direction. Doug was out there somewhere. He had to find him. Put a stop to this once and for all.

A dark figure, about Doug's size, ran across the intersection and a driver honked his horn. Todd ran after him, careful not to be seen. The figure ran into a bookstore. Todd took a deep gulp of air to calm himself and then went in after him.

The store was bright and silent, as if sound didn't exist in this place. Todd didn't like it. It was preternatural. Like something out of The Twilight Zone.

Todd crept up and down the aisles searching for his prey. Nothing. He climbed the stairs, careful to keep a look out. And there, turning the corner of the next aisle in the history section. The same umber slacks and jacket. The same white shirt.

Todd waited until Doug disappeared behind the shelf, pondering his next move. Club Doug on the back of the head with the biggest book he could find?

That would never do. He'd follow Doug, see where it led. Todd risked a peek, curling his fingers around the bookshelf. He looked.

A figure looked back at him.

Todd jumped.

"You okay?" A man was smiling. A man in umber slacks. A man that was not Doug.

Todd faltered and shook his head. "Yes. I'm okay. You surprised me." In more ways than the guy knew. The man nodded and returned his attention to a book on Civil War history. A finger tapped Todd between the shoulder blades. Todd screamed and turned.

"Can I help you?" A middle-aged woman in a billowy gray dress was looking up at him. There was a store ID pinned to her reasonably flat chest. "Is there a problem?"

"No, no problem." Todd hurried out the store. Think, he told himself. If I were Doug, where would I be?

Todd cursed. The answer wasn't pleasant. Where he'd be was out looking to gun Todd down.

How was that revelation going to help Todd now?

Todd wandered aimlessly up the street, eyes barely registering the people that he passed.

Happy, and probably drunken, shouts coming from the Hooters restaurant located on the third floor of CocoWalk, the Grove's premiere shopping and entertainment complex, which Todd was now passing along caused him to look up. Just ahead, a hip-looking panhandler in an eggplant Ralph Lauren polo shirt had his hand out. The man he was accosting slapped it away.

Doug.

And Todd had nearly run right smack into him. Todd backpedaled and stepped into the doorway of Banana Republic. Yes, it was Doug.

Todd grinned a toothless grin. Gotcha, he thought.

Todd stuck to Doug like a second shadow. Doug roamed with no apparent aim in mind for an hour, stopping to look in shop windows now and again. The first time Doug had done so, Todd realized with horror that Doug might spot his reflection in the glass. Afterward, he was careful to stay far out of the light, not ever losing sight of the mad doctor.

Doug stopped for a drink at a packed hole in the wall bar on a quiet sidestreet. He ordered a second, then a third. Finally, Doug staggered out into the night, unbuttoning the top button of his shirt as he shuffled up the sidewalk. Todd ducked into the dark entryway of a closed leather goods shop and turned his back to the door as Doug passed close.

Todd gave Doug a few steps head start, then followed. It wasn't long before Doug's newest destination became apparent. It was the Coconut Grove Boat Club out on South

Bayshore Drive. Todd recalled that Doug was a member.

Todd kept his distance and watched as Doug stumbled along the dock to his boat, a 2001 Sea Ray 360 Sundancer. Not too big, but a beauty. Todd had had his eye on getting a boat for some time before buying a Sea Ray himself, a '95 Sea Ray 380 Sundancer that he picked up secondhand and kept in dry dock at his Port Lauderdale condo. Boat slips were tough to come by and his condo building had its own brand new, state-of-the-art, computerized dry dock system, a parking garage for boats up to fifty-five foot in length. They could drop Todd's boat in the water in seven minutes.

That had been one of the reasons he'd bought in the building. Not to mention, Port Lauderdale was going to be a great investment. He'd stay a few more years, then cash in, get a fifty-percent return on his investment, if all went well and the stock market remained in the toilet.

Todd leaned against a palm tree, feeling the rush of warm wind blowing through his shirt. Doug climbed over the rail. A light went on inside.

Another light went on, this one inside Todd's head.

Spotting a lone payphone out at the edge of the parking lot, he dug into his pocket for loose change and the remnants of Det. Durham's business card. It was several minutes before a voice answered. Todd was relieved that the fuzzy voice on the other end did not belong to Durham's wife.

"Hello, it's Todd."

"What's up?"

"I'm in Miami. *He's* here." A sudden surge of paranoia kept Todd from uttering Doug's name. "On his boat."

There was a long, fuzzy silence. Finally, Durham said,

"Okay. That could work."

The detective spoke some more, prodded Todd about the boat. He seemed very interested in it for some reason. Todd gave a detailed description of Doug's vessel, *Dr. Doug's Dream*, and told him the slip number where it was docked.

Durham grunted and told Todd to go home. Todd was only too happy to agree and gave the detective directions to the marina.

:14

Todd stared at his watch. It was after eleven. Shit. Holly was going to kill him!

He ran all the way back to Senor Frog's. Todd was sheathed in perspiration when he arrived. To his surprise, the table he and Holly had occupied was now home to a fifty-something Latino couple and their two sleepy-eyed children.

He found his waitress inside. She didn't know anything. Only that the young lady he was with had gone.

Todd squeezed his eyes shut and groaned. She really was going to murder him. He headed back up into the heart of the Grove with ever-quickening steps. There was no sign of Holly. He even tried the nightclubs, hoping she might be waiting for him inside one.

The illuminated clock in a burger joint announced that it was nearly midnight. Wearily, Todd headed for his car. He had to face it, Holly had gone. Probably caught a cab. He winced. A cab to Fort Lauderdale was going to be very pricey. He'd have to pay her back for that.

Todd crossed the street and laid his arms across the valet

stand behind which a scruffy, pock-marked kid in denim jeans and T-shirt sat in a folding chair listening to an MP3 player. "Silver BMW," Todd said wearily, reaching in his pants for the ticket stub.

The kid pulled his earphones down around his neck and waited.

Todd frowned. He'd given the stub to Holly. She'd stuck it in her purse. "I must have lost it."

The kid's frown matched his own. The boy stood. "You got some ID?"

"Sure." Todd produced his wallet.

The kid looked at it and shrugged. "Which one of 'em is yours?"

The lot, a school parking lot by day, was dark, but Todd remembered the kid parked it along the fence under one of those big trees whose roots were slowly eating away at the blacktop. He squinted. "Should be right over there." He traced a line along the length of the fence. His eyes retraced the route.

It should be over there, but it wasn't.

"I-I don't see it," Todd stammered. Shit. Had his car been stolen? Could anything else in his life go wrong?

"What kind of vehicle were you driving, buddy?"

Todd ignored his first impulse, which was to tell this punk that he was not his buddy, and described the car.

The kid nodded. "Cool. No problem. Your wife already took it." He scratched his thigh.

"My wife?"

"Yeah. She's hot, mister. But what happened? She was all messed up. You two get in a food fight?"

Todd stared at the kid wishing he had the nerve to slug him. Holly had taken his car. *His* car!

Todd walked until he found a payphone, stuck in a quarter and dialed his car phone. No answer except for his own cheerful and professional sounding voicemail message. "Fuck you, Todd Jones," he hissed into the phone, letting the mouthpiece drop. It spun around uselessly at the end of its cord, a metaphor for the way Todd himself was feeling about his own predicament.

Holly was probably home now, curled up in her nice, warm, oversized bed. Exactly where he expected to be about this time. Instead he was alone, in Coconut Grove. Without wheels.

Todd worried about his BMW. He only hoped it wasn't at the bottom of some canal by now. The way Holly was probably feeling about him, it wouldn't surprise Todd if that was exactly where his 540i was resting now, holding its breath till morning. Probably be a couple of alligators making out in the backseat.

Todd looked at his watch and rubbed his wrist. Durham should be arriving soon. Todd came to the decision that he might as well stick around. He wandered back to the marina and planted himself on a bus bench beside the road.

He was tired. More tired now that he'd sat down and the day had begun to catch up with him. Todd closed his dry, aching eyes, let his chin rest against his chest and waited. The salty breeze coming in off the bay made him long for the islands. Maybe he'd go on down to the Bahamas when this was all over, or St. Martin maybe. . .

Something kicked his foot. Todd broke free of his dream.

He and Holly had been at some celebrity function up in Palm Beach at one of those big coral rock mansions along the Atlantic. The walls had come alive, transforming into rock monsters that attacked everyone in sight, demanding their home back. He and Holly were running, fighting for their lives. There was the sound of broken glass as they busted through a gigantic plate glass window in the study. A yellow Porsche was waiting outside. Holly yelled Run! But Todd was afraid to go near the car. A gargantuan rock monster shaped like a dragon came swooping through the air. Fire shot from its mouth.

Todd screamed. He felt a mild throbbing in his foot.

"I thought I told you to go home." The monster hovered over him, its pulsating, red-stained eyes only inches from his own. Todd's pupils adjusted to the darkness and the foreign surroundings. It was Detective Durham. Not a monster at all.

Todd swallowed hard. His throat was dry. He felt the bench with his hands. Yes, he was on a bus stop bench. In Coconut Grove. It wasn't a rock monster. It was Nicholas Durham. Nickelodeon Man. "Hey, Nick."

Durham planted his hands on his hips. He wore black Nikes, brown sweatpants and a loose, short-sleeved charcoal sweater. He didn't look too awake himself. "You okay? You having second thoughts?"

Todd struggled to his feet. His legs were numb from sitting. He massaged his upper thighs with his knuckles. "No, not at all." He explained what had happened with his girlfriend.

Durham snorted. "Women. We sure can pick 'em, can't we?"

91

Todd could only agree. "She left with my car." Todd looked up and down the street. "Speaking of which, where's your car?"

"Public lot near the boat club. Come on, let's go."

Todd pulled the detective's sleeve. "You came alone, didn't you?"

"What do you think?"

"Sorry. Stupid question, eh?"

"Yeah. Now let's get down to business. I've got a dirty dozen waiting for us in my car."

Todd had to measure his steps to keep pace with the slow shuffling detective. Dirty dozen? What the hell had Durham brought?

Thugs? Machine guns? Incendiary devices?

They climbed in Durham's Chevy and the detective angled the vehicle towards the bobbing boats in the marina. Together, they stared through the windshield. The sounds of a party, music and laughter, came from a yacht at the end of the farthest dock. Everything else was quiet.

Durham reached over into the backseat and came up with a twelve back of Bud. "Meet the dirty dozen."

Todd wrapped his hand around a still cold bottle. Nonlethal, but plenty welcome nonetheless. He quenched his nagging thirst gratefully. "That's Doug's Sundancer over there." Todd aimed the bottle toward slip number 18B.

"Nice." Durham reached for a fresh bottle and tossed one Todd's way as well. "Gas, you say?"

"That's right. Twin MerCruiser gas V-drives."

"I'm surprised he didn't go for diesel. Safer."

"Tell me about it. I've got a pre-owned   Sundancer

myself, 38 footer, with diesel. I'm not taking any chances."
Todd had heard all the lectures at his Coast Guard boating
skills and seamanship classes. Gas in the bilges can explode.
Diesel can't. There was more to it than that, he was sure, but
that was all he remembered. That was enough.

"That's smart." Durham made sucking noises, his lips
clenched to his Bud like a baby hungrily suckling a teat. "I'd
say your friend isn't."

Todd smiled. "Doug's cheap. That's one of his many
problems."

The detective nodded ever so slightly. Durham had
tipped his seat back and shut his eyes, his beer cradled in his
hands, resting against his chest like a month-old baby.

Todd furrowed his brow. "What do we do now?"

Durham rolled his head in Todd's direction and opened
one eye. "We wait." The eye fell shut.

Todd stared out the dirt-streaked, moth and lovebug
spattered windshield at *Dr. Doug's Dream* wondering what the
hell kind of nightmare he'd gotten himself into.

:15

Durham nudged Todd awake. "That him?"

Todd stretched. He opened his eyes and winced. The brilliant yellow-orange sun was torching the intense blue sky. How could anything that far away be that powerful? Surely the astronomers were wrong. The damn thing had to be a lot closer to earth than ninety-three million miles. A helluva lot closer.

He put a hand up to shade his eyes and Durham knocked it back down. "Keep out of sight." Durham scrunched down to the level of the steering wheel. "So, is that him?"

Todd watched the doughy man in baggy shorts and a white polo shirt as he stood on the deck with what looked like a steaming cup of coffee in his hands. "That's him." Todd squeezed his eyes almost shut. A high-powered rifle with a laser scope and he could take care of his problem right then and there.

Todd turned to the detective. "What are we going to do next?"

Durham looked amused. "*We* aren't going to do

anything." He jabbed a blunt-ended index finger at Todd. "*You* are going home."

"You're kidding, right?" Todd twisted his shoulder. Every bone, muscle and sinew in his body was aching and stiff. Sleeping in cars was not his idea of a good time. Especially when Doug was living the good life on his boat mere yards away.

"I'm kidding, wrong." The bottom half of Durham's face had sprouted an amount of hair that for Todd would have been impossible in four full days let alone one short night. "He knows you. He spots you, it's over." Durham rubbed his neck. "No element of surprise."

Surprise. Right. He liked that. Give Dr. Doug a taste of his own medicine.

Todd watched Doug as he came up the dock heading for town. They dug themselves down deeper into the Chevy, practically squeezing themselves up under the clunky dashboard.

Stealing a peek a moment later, they saw Doug turn in to a busy breakfast joint.

Durham reached across and opened Todd's door. "Okay, out you go."

"Wait," said Todd, "I don't have a car. How am I going to get home?"

Durham cursed. "Okay. New plan." He shook his head with apparent disgust. "I hate that, when a plan changes. But okay. Get back in."

Todd gratefully hauled his butt back inside the oppressive Chevy.

"You take my car."

Todd could almost see the detective's gears turning.

"There's a shopping center up near Gulfstream Park. Southeast corner. You know the place?"

Todd nodded. Gulfstream Park race track. Shopping center. "No problem."

"Leave the car in the lot. Leave the passenger door unlocked and the key in the ashtray." He jiggled the key in the ignition for emphasis and popped open the ashtray.

It was full of gum wrappers and foreign-looking gook. Todd wondered how he'd stuff the key in all that gunk without getting any of it on his fingers.

"I'll pick the Chevy up later. You'll have to catch a cab to your place from there." Durham slid between the front seats and out the back passenger side door, careful to keep out of sight of the restaurant.

Durham crawled around the car and popped the trunk open, pulled something out and then pushed the lid back down. "Later."

Todd's stiff fingers clutched the hard steering wheel. He watched the detective's hunched over figure loping towards the dock. One hand carried a bright red gas can with a yellow nozzle.

Todd wanted to scream "then what?" but it was too late. Durham was too far away, a distant, puzzling crab of a man with a can full of gasoline.

Todd squeezed his temples between his thumb and his middle finger. Why didn't he simply step on the accelerator and ram the Chevy through the big plate glass window of that breakfast joint? With luck, Doug would be sitting in one of the booths along the window.

End of story.

So a few bystanders would die. They'd understand.

Instead, Todd started up the big engine and headed for Gulfstream Park up in Hallandale Beach. Gulfstream was a horse track. The main track was a one-mile oval that had absorbed a good deal of Todd's money over the years. He'd had better luck on the turf track. Any other time, he'd consider placing a wager or two while he was there.

But not this time.

Not the way his luck was running these days

.

:16

Too wired to sleep and anxious for someone to talk to, Todd dropped Durham's Chevy off in a space under the Gulfstream Shopping Center sign and caught a cab to Doug and Caroline Freeman's house.

One good thing had come of the trip up from Miami, he'd passed a sign for clean fill along the freeway and made a note of it. Todd had stuck the scrap of paper in his pocket. He'd call the number Monday. Maybe get Constantine off his back. That would already be something.

The Freeman's Intracoastal home was in Aventura, not far south of Hallandale. A five minute taxi ride. With Doug in Coconut Grove, Todd had nothing to worry about. He'd go see Caroline, get her take on the situation and Doug's frame of mind.

Not that it mattered much anymore.

The cab dropped him off in front. There was no sign of a yellow Carrera but it could have been tucked away behind any one of the four garage doors. Todd paid off the driver and rang the bell, shaking off his fears. The smell of roses and jasmine filled the shaded entry. Aromatherapy for his jangly nerves.

Todd told himself that it was unlikely that Doug was home. Though Doug could have beat him here if he wanted to. Such thoughts were not worth thinking. Todd saw Caroline's graceful figure, wrapped in a blue and white pareo and white bikini top, through the glass. She looked surprised to see him, but waved from the foyer.

Caroline opened the door. "Todd, what are you doing here?"

Todd noticed her eyes looking up and down the quiet street. "We've got to talk." His life was churning up inside him like sour milk. He needed somebody he could be honest with, open up to. The way he figured, that somebody was Caroline. They were in this together, after all.

Caroline told him to come inside. Her bare feet made no sound on the cool marble floor as he followed her swaying hips out to the pool deck. "Doug's not here."

"I know. That's what I want to talk to you about."

"Coffee?" She held a delicate porcelain coffee pitcher in one slender fingered hand.

Todd nodded and she went to the outdoor bar, returned with a second cup and filled it. "Thanks." He watched her breathe, her breasts rising and falling like twin temptations. Beneath that skimpy material he knew he'd find no tan lines. Caroline wasn't one for white lines.

"What's this about Doug?"

Todd came back to earth, remembered that if he wanted to survive he had to think with his big head, not his little one. "He knows about us. He's trying to kill me."

Caroline gazed steadily out at the water. She was a long time replying. "That's ridiculous."

Todd shook his head. The caffeine was doing its job. He felt himself coming to life. A wondrous condition he planned on keeping as long as possible. Another fifty years minimum. "No, it's not. I'm telling you. Doug knows. He confronted me when I went for my checkup the other night. You didn't tell him, did you?"

"Don't be silly, Todd." One corner of Caroline's full and potent lips turned up, as if she found this all very amusing. "What did he say exactly?"

"He said that he knew we'd slept together."

Her lips grew into a smile.

"And he gave me five minutes to live."

Caroline outright laughed, bringing her hand to her face, her ten-ton wedding ring glittering brightly in the sunlight. "That's wonderful."

Todd's eyes grew wide. "Wonderful? Your maniac husband is trying to kill me for sleeping with his wife and you think that's wonderful?"

Her bare, sensuous shoulders shrugged. "I don't mean it like that, baby." She leaned forward.

Todd smelled cocoa butter. He loved cocoa butter.

"Don't you see?"

Todd didn't.

"Doug knows. About us. That means we don't have to hide what we're doing any longer. We're free to do as we please."

Todd was looking at her as if she'd just stated that the world was flat and that the two of them were standing on the wrong side of it, upside down, like a couple of bats. Caroline was batty, that was for sure.

Like her batty husband.

He smothered a groan. What the hell had he gotten himself into? All he'd wanted was to have a little fun, for crying out loud. "He's trying to kill me, Caroline. Get it? He shot a fucking gun at me. He wants me dead."

Caroline shook her head, long blonde hair, fine as a baby's, courtesy of her colorist no doubt, tickled her cheeks before settling down. "He wouldn't dare."

Her hands went up. "He wouldn't want to lose all this. And he can't make a big stink about you and me because then he knows I'll raise a fuss over all the little cunts he's slept with over the years. And he's absolutely terrified of the D word."

"Divorce."

Caroline, nodded, looking positively thrilled with her life. "Believe me, baby, the idea of alimony scares Doug more than death itself."

Todd protested. "You didn't see him, Caroline. I've known Doug for years and I've never seen him like this. He's nuts. And he's trying to kill me." He replayed several close calls and told how Doug had been stalking him.

Caroline only found this all the more amusing. "Don't you see, baby, he's playing with you. Trying to scare you off." Caroline stood and released the knot in her pareo. Mile long legs and a perfect tush barely concealed in a white Rio thong practically turned Todd to jelly. "You've got balls, don't you?" She reached between his legs and squeezed, smiled.

Todd gulped, tried to nod.

"Be a man, Todd. Use them." Caroline reached into his pants and came out with a prize.

"Caroline, this is not a good idea. Doug—"

"Fuck Doug," replied Caroline, pulling Todd into the house. "Better yet," she said, pushing him down on the deep leather sofa in the living room with her free hand, "fuck me."

:17

"Thanks for the ride." Todd's hand went to the door handle.

Her eyes sparkled mischievously. "Thank *you* for the ride, cowboy."

"Listen," began Todd, "maybe we should take it easy for a while."

"You still worried about Doug, Todd? Forget about my husband," Caroline said. "I'm sure this whole thing will blow over."

Todd blocked his thoughts. Was Caroline reading his mind? 'Blow over' was just too appropriate. His left hand stroked the supple tan leather seat of Caroline's 760Li. She had parked in the meager shade provided by a cluster of king palms outside his Port Lauderdale condo. "You may be right."

"Of course, I'm right. If you ask me, Doug is madder at you for getting him into that Kendall deal than he is with you for getting into my underwear." Her fingers did a little dance across Todd's chest.

He felt himself getting aroused all over again. That was not good. He needed to behave himself. Fooling around had become a deadly past-time. Right then and there, he made a silent vow to behave himself in the future.

"That little investment's lost him over a quarter of a million last year alone and Doug says it's still losing money." Caroline's hand slid into his shirt and fingers scampered freely. "Have I mentioned that money is all Doug cares about?"

Todd pulled her hand away. "If he'd only be more patient. I still think that place could make some serious money."

That place was Kendall Kastles, a time share condominium, one hundred and fifty new units in the city of Kendall. So far, they'd managed to sell less than twenty-percent of the units. That meant the investors were forced to carry heavy loans for the construction and maintenance of the property. Todd had lost fifty grand himself before selling out. The fact that he had gotten out, he kept a well-guarded secret from the others.

Who knew nobody wanted time shares in Kendall? At the time Todd had gotten Doug and the other dozen investors involved, there had been talk of a championship golf club in the area and a new waterpark, like Seaquarium but with rollercoasters. Todd had told the investors they'd be getting in early and would soon be cleaning up.

Neither the golf course nor the waterpark had panned out. The only other new development had been a strip mall with a Dunkin Donuts shop and Payless Shoes.

Thank goodness Constantine wasn't one of the Kendall

Kastles investors, though Todd had initially tried to lure him into the deal. Todd suppressed a shiver. He would be frying in olive oil by now.

The phone in Caroline's purse began chirping. "I'd better get that. It's probably Doug. Call me later, okay?"

"Look, about Doug—"

She held the phone in one hand, looking expectantly at Todd. "Yes?"

Should he tell her the rest? That he'd planned on murdering Doug before Doug murdered him? Todd crushed his fist into his opposite hand. No, he couldn't. Though she professed no love for her husband, she might find feelings for Doug buried deep inside her come rushing to the surface if she discovered that he was in trouble. And that would spell more Todd trouble.

Besides, nothing was sure yet. "Forget it."

Caroline took her foot off the brake and silently drove away. Todd could see she was talking on the phone. Was she speaking to Doug? Or was it only possible to speak with Dr. Delirious as a disembodied voice now?

All this waiting and wondering was driving Todd crazy. He ignored the doorman's greeting and marched up to his condo.

The phone was ringing impatiently when he stepped inside. "Hello?"

"Todd, it's me."

"Mother?"

"How are you, baby?"

Todd groaned. "This is not a good time, Mother. Can I call you back?" Todd's mom had gotten as fed up with

Detroit's winters as Todd. She wanted to move down to Florida, closer to her one and only child. Fearing he'd be smothered with his mother's love, Todd had convinced her that Naples was more her style and had helped her buy a nice oceanfront condo there. That had been two years ago and, so far, the arrangement was working and his mother seemed happy. But now was not a good time for a phone call.

Her raspy, cigarette-ravaged laughter drilled into his delicate ear bones. "No, you can't call me back. What you can do is to tell this young fellow here to let me up."

Todd squeezed the bridge of his nose. A tornado-like headache was coming to life and he valiantly, if vainly, tried to squelch it. "Let you up?" Was some guy sitting on his mother?

"Yes, I'm down in the lobby and this young man says he has orders to let no one up. Not even your own mother? What kind of place is this you're living in, Todd, baby?"

"You're in the lobby? My lobby?" Todd's headache twisted out of control, knocking down the barn and threatening the main house and the silo. There go the crops, Ma.

She laughed a second time. "Surprise, surprise. Thought I'd come pay you a visit. Now, you going to tell this young man here to let me up?"

Todd told his mother to give the phone to the doorman. "Hello?"

"Good morning, Mr. Jones. It's me, Carlos."

"Carlos? What are you doing on the day shift?"

"Filling in for Guillermo. His wife's having a baby."

"Again?" Todd smothered a yawn. "You'd better let her

up.

"No problem. I'll bring Mrs. Jones up myself. She'll need help with her bags."

Bags? Todd groaned. As he hung up, he heard his mother yelling at poor Carlos that she didn't need any help at all.

Todd bounced around the living room and kitchen straightening as best he could. The doorbell rang and he ran to answer it. "Hello, M—" He looked over his mother's shoulder. There was Det. Durham, standing behind his mother like an afterthought. And Carlos the doorman was standing against the wall with a couple of purple suitcases.

"Hi, Todd."

"Detec-I mean, Nick, what a surprise." His eyes sought answers. "What are you doing here?"

"I was in the neighborhood and thought I'd stop by. I was hoping we could talk some business. I didn't realize that your mother was arriving. Maybe I should come back another time."

"Nonsense. Stay. Mr. Durham and I met in the lobby, Todd." Mrs. Jones hugged her son. She smelled of Camels and White Shoulders by Elizabeth Arden, a not-unpleasant concoction of gardenia, neroli oil, jasmine and musk on most women, but a pungent spewing of toxins when mixed with his mother's natural body oils. She'd been smoking and perfuming practically her whole life, at least that part of it that Todd shared. "Put the bags down already, Carlos. You want you should get a hernia?"

Carlos placed the bags inside the door and winked at Todd. On his way out, he wished Mrs. Jones a pleasant stay.

Mrs. Jones said to the detective, "You want to buy a

house?"

"Yes, ma'am."

She looked down her nose at him. "You don't look like you can afford it. You ought to dress better. Get yourself groomed."

"Mother!"

"What? I'm only trying to help the man." Mrs. Jones turned to Durham. "My son's the best. He'll find you someplace affordable and clean." She sighed and clapped her hands. "I'm going to wash up."

"Yes, Mother." Todd rolled his eyes for Durham's benefit then hauled his mother's bags to the guest room on the opposite side of the apartment. He shut the door behind her, wishing he could lock her in.

"That'll give us a little time." Todd poured himself and Nick Durham a couple of generous scotches from the wet bar. "No offense, but Mother's right. You look like hell. Tell me quick. What happened?"

The detective took his time responding, slowly relishing his drink. "You try stowing away in a boat after spending the night in your car and see how you come out looking and smelling."

Todd nodded, finished his glass.

"I had a little trouble. Had to wait a bit for the sonofabitch to eat his breakfast. Not that he needed the nourishment."

Todd allowed himself a smile. "You mean—"

Durham nodded. "It didn't go exactly as planned, but it went. "You can read the good news in tomorrow's paper. Enjoy it. Most days the news is lousy."

Todd stared out the window past the balcony, savoring his pricey view of the water and the detective's words of his salvation. "Fuck you, Doug. You wanted me dead and it's you that's meeting your maker, whomever that may be. May the Devil take you, Doug Freeman." He pictured the deceased doctor, all million bits of him, floating around in Key Biscayne.

Todd slowly refilled their glasses and raised his in a toast. "To success."

Durham clinked his glass against Todd's. "And gasoline."

Todd laughed, choked on his scotch, and wiped his mouth with a cold hand.

"I've never killed anybody before," Durham said. "It's kind of weird. But even while I was splashing gas down in the bilge and around the engines, I didn't feel too bad about it."

"We do what we have to do to preserve ourselves and our lives."

"And don't forget, to improve our lot."

Todd nodded. "I haven't forgotten. I'll get you your money."

"When?"

Todd chewed his lip, set his empty tumbler on the black granite counter. "The beginning of the week. You trust me, don't you?"

Durham shook his head. "No. But I took the precaution of taping a couple of our conversations." He patted a bulge in his shirt pocket. "In case anything goes wrong."

"I see."

"They always say you can never have too much insurance."

Todd felt a wave of sweat threatening to break from beneath every pore of his skin. A million little boys and a million fingers were going to be called up from the reserves to plug the million plus holes in the dike that was Todd Jones. "Nothing will go wrong."

He hoped.

:18

Todd saw Durham out, then tiptoed to the guestroom door and silently pushed his ear up against it. Sounded like Mom was taking a shower and hacking her way through an unmellifluous rendition of the Talking Heads' *Burning Down The House*. Mom had always had peculiar taste in music for a woman of her generation.

Todd got the coffee pot started and headed to his room.

"Yo, bro'."

Todd screeched to a halt, practically tearing up the wool carpet and burning the soles of his feet.

"Steve!" Todd took a quick look over his shoulder. Mother was nowhere in sight. "What are you doing here?" Steve lay stretched out on Todd's king-size bed, his scruffy hair resting against the saffron upholstered headboard. That headboard had set him back fifteen-hundred bucks. Steve was barefoot and bare chested. A fashionably frazzled pair of jeans covered his legs.

Steve grinned. "Man, you're one brutal dude, bro'." Steve sat up and uncrossed his ankles. "Who'd you kill?"

"What?" stuttered Todd.

"A cop? A girlfriend?" Steve seemed to enjoy the guessing game. "Your wife?"

"I didn't kill anybody," Todd stammered. "How'd you get in here, anyway?"

"Come off it, man." That stupid grin never left Steve's face. "I heard you talking. What'd you do, torch some guy? Why didn't you use the gun I gave you? It was loaded, for chrissakes. A hell of a lot simpler and surer than flame-broiling a guy." His brow arched wickedly. "Or a girl."

"I didn't flame-broil anybody."

"I heard you talking to some guy out there." Steve jumped off the bed and draped an arm over Todd's shoulder. "Don't worry," he cooed. "We're friends. Buds. I ain't gonna squeal on you."

He lightly punched Todd in the arm. "We're on the same team." Steve drilled his index fingers along each side of his skull like a couple of Frankensteinian monster-like bolts. "We think the same."

Todd doubted that. He doubted that very much. Steve was wacko. Todd pulled away. He shut the bedroom door. He contemplated tossing Steve out the bedroom window but knew that even if he could overpower the kid, he didn't have the character for the task. "My mother's in the other room. She's come for a visit. Now is not a good time."

Steve nodded and scooped up an open can of Pepsi from the night table. "I understand. Look, whatever you did, don't worry. I've got your ass covered. I'll say you were home all night and that I was here with you."

Todd watched Steve's Adam's apple bounce up and down

as he drank.

"That much is true, anyway."

"I don't need an alibi. I didn't do anything." Todd went to the bathroom and turned on the cold water faucet, splashing his face. "You never did say how you got in here."

Steve checked a pimple in the mirror. "Easy. I called the doorman saying I was you and to let Steve Brezhinski up."

Todd groaned. So much for security. Any simpleton could figure out a way around a human being. Maybe the next condo he moved into he'd make sure they had computerized security guards. Maybe armed robots.

Todd toweled his face and hands. "Okay. Why?"

"Why what?"

"Why did you do that? Why are you here, Steve?"

"Needed a place to crash. Pop's mad at me for getting the car shot up again."

Again? Somehow Todd wasn't surprised.

"Thought I'd hang out here and cool it for a couple of days."

Todd grabbed Steve's upper arm. "Listen, Steve." Steve was wiping his teeth in the mirror with the side of his index finger. "Are you listening?"

Steve nodded.

"Steve, you can't stay here. Now is not a good time. I mean, any other time, that would be great. But not now. My mother is visiting. Who knows how long she'll stay?"

Surfer Steve pulled his finger out of his mouth. "That's cool. I gotcha. Tough break." He grabbed his shirt off the chair opposite Todd's bed. "Guess I'll go home and check out the situation. Pop's had a night to calm down. He never stays mad too long. I'll pick him up a case of his favorite brandy."

Steve stuck his foot in one sandal and rummaged around for the other. He found it underneath the bed and slipped it on.

Todd marched him to the door after looking to see that the coast was clear.

Steve said he'd call Todd later and check on him. See if there's anything Todd needed.

"That really isn't necessary, Steve."

"My pleasure, dude. And when you're ready to talk," he thumped his chest, "I'm here to listen." Steve dropped his voice. "I know what it's like to kill a man."

A chill ran through Todd. He couldn't wait for Steve to get the hell out of his apartment and was glad when the crazy kid crossed the threshold. Of course, Todd figured he'd have to get his lock changed.

Steve pressed the call button for the elevators and turned in Todd's direction. "Remember, bro', I'm here for you." Steve gave Todd the old thumbs-up. "Like this morning when that guy called you. What a prick. I gave him something to think about."

The ping! of the elevator announced its arrival. Todd padded into the hall. "What guy?"

Steve stepped into the box. "I dunno. Some fool calling himself Aristotle."

Surfer Steve's hand pressed L for lobby. "Can you imagine? Who the fuck does he think he is, a goddamn philosopher? And calling on a Sunday morning no less. What a jerk." Steve chuckled. "Well, I gave his old ass something to philosophize over."

The door started to slide shut. Todd jumped in front of it, hands first. The doors snapped against his wrists then receded. Todd cried out in pain.

Steve looked at him like he was crazy. "What'd you go and do that for?"

Todd grabbed the kid by the collar. "That was Aristotle Constantine that called."

Steve scratched the side of his head. "Yeah, that could've been it. That might be what he said."

Todd's jaw was clamped tight and the words barely came through. "What else did he say?"

"He said he wanted to know about his dirt and when he was going to get it and what it was going to cost. Shit like that." Steve looked at Todd's hands. "You're ripping my shirt, dude."

Todd loosened his grip. The elevator doors had shut and Todd could feel them hurtling near silently towards earth. "What else did he say?"

Steve shrugged. "Not much. I didn't much like his tone of voice. I told him to go fuck himself. Told him next time he called hassling one of my friends that he was gonna get himself a thirty-eight caliber nose job."

Todd's jaw dropped like the lid of a big dumpster. More appropriate still, the lid of a coffin. Not just any coffin, his coffin. "You didn't—"

Steve chuckled. "Oh, yeah. You should've heard him start cursing after that." The elevator opened at ground level and Steve stepped out.

Todd's hands had dropped to his sides. He held the

elevator open with his bare foot. "Then what?" Todd didn't even know why he'd bothered to ask. Did he really want to know?

"I hung up on him." Steve pointed a gnarly finger at Todd. "Call you later, bro'."

:19

Todd didn't even see him coming.

One minute the elevator door was closing. The next minute he was alone in the elevator with Thug Peter.

Todd sucked in his breath. The small elevator seemed suddenly ten sizes smaller.

Peter nestled in real close. His breath reeked of toasted Spanish almonds. "Mr. Constantine's not real happy with you, Mr. Jones."

Todd opened his mouth but Peter put a finger to his lips. "He don't like people disrespecting him. Says maybe you need to learn some manners."

"I wasn't disrespecting him, Peter. Honest." Todd pointed. "It was that crazy kid out there. You must have seen him in the lobby." Todd talked fast. The elevator was on its way up.

"I saw him."

"He broke into my apartment. I was out all night. Caught him in there this morning and kicked him out."

"The two of you looked awfully chummy to me, Mr.

Jones."

"Chummy? Are you kidding?" Todd looked pleadingly at Peter. "He's some nutjob. That's all. I swear." He placed his right hand over his heart.

The elevator doors opened back up on Todd's floor and Peter escorted Todd to his unit.

Thug Peter went to open the door and Todd stopped him. "My mother's inside."

Peter paused and chewed his lip. "You sure?"

Todd nodded. "Showed up. A surprise visit. That's how I was able to get that nutjob out." He turned the handle. "See for yourself."

Peter glanced inside but his feet stayed in the hall. "You got a name on that insolent kid?"

"No. I don't even know how he managed to get in the building. Some security, eh?"

Peter's eyes bored holes through Todd's flesh reducing him to Swiss cheese. "You see him again, you tell him nobody speaks to Aristotle Constantine like he did. You tell him he's got to apologize. Offer Mr. Constantine a present," said Peter in a soft yet dangerous voice, "like a kidney or his nose."

Todd promised. Before Thug Peter had even half-turned, Todd was behind the door and the lock was bolted. He leaned against the door for a minute, taking quick, shallow breaths that gradually slowed to a human rate.

He spent the day entertaining his mother and slept fitfully. His mind swimming with images of death and destruction, mostly his own. But some were Doug. Somewhere in the middle of the night he woke in a chill sweat. The sheets were soaked through and he tossed them off, spending the rest of the night on the bare mattress.

He woke bleary-eyed and weak, but filled with determination and a renewed sense of self. With his mother all geared up for a day of flea market shopping, Todd's schedule was his own.

And this was going to be one good day. If Durham had done his job right. The future was all roses. He sniffed the heady bouquet of his rebirth. The future smelled so good he decided to forego the antiperspirant this morning.

Todd put on his medium blue suit, the one that made him look ten pounds thinner and christened a new white shirt. He kept a neat stack of them in a lower drawer of his walk-in closet. Down in the lobby of his building, he said good morning to the doorman on duty and stuffed a couple of quarters into the news vending machine.

Reading over the top edges of his sunglasses, Todd grinned. It was all right there. Front page of the local section, below the fold.

Boat Explosion Kills One.

Prominent local physician, Douglas F. Freeman, died early Sunday morning in a boating incident which, according to a Miami Coast Guard spokesperson, was likely caused by improper ventilation or other engine trouble yet to be determined. Witnesses report hearing a loud explosion which rocked the marina, followed by the sight of flames. The vessel, Dr. Doug's Dream, was totally destroyed. The doctor's body has yet to be recovered, though search efforts continue.

Blah blah blah.

Todd's eyes scanned the rest of the story. *Survived by his wife, Caroline. . .Practice in Ft. Lauderdale. . .No children. . .*

Boring. One more accident in a world full of accidents. Happens every day.

Todd tossed the paper in the trash.

He picked up a car over at a rental agency in Pompano where he knew the owner, having helped him with the purchase of the land and building, bought a new cellphone at Circuit City and made it to his office by ten o'clock.

Todd thought about calling Holly—he hadn't seen or heard from her since Saturday night—but first things first. He pulled the scrap of paper from his wallet with the name and number of the place selling clean fill.

He explained his problem to a guy named Jack who promised to run up and have a look at the property in question and get back to him with an estimate. "Sounds like a lot of water," commented Jack. "Sounds like you're going to need a lot of fill."

Todd tracked Mr. Constantine down at one of his businesses, a restaurant down in North Miami Beach, and related the good news. Constantine sounded somewhat appeased, or maybe it was the fact that he was on his third ouzo of the day.

He spent the next couple of hours catching up with clients and tracking sales. Feeling good and hungry, Todd climbed into his loaner, a red Sebring convertible and headed to Holly's place of employment, Sunshine Savings and Loan, the branch over on Oakland Park Boulevard.

She gave him the cold shoulder when he dropped down in the chair across from her desk. He slid his hand across her desk and she rolled back. "Hiya, babe. You look great. Hungry?" Did she know about Doug Freeman yet? There were no signs of crying visible around her eyes.

"Yes."

"Great. How about that Chinese joint over on Andrews?"
No balled up tissues tossed about her desk.

"I'm busy."

Todd frowned. Holly wasn't one for reading the
newspaper. Of course, Caroline might have called Holly and
dropped the news bomb. "Listen, Hol, I'm really sorry about
Saturday night. It's this Doug thing. He's got me worried. I've
never seen him acting so strangely."

Todd gave her a conspiratorial look. "I think he may be
suicidal. I wonder if I should talk to Caroline about it?"

There, he'd brought up Caroline's name. How would
Holly respond? He congratulated himself on the suicide
angle. Maybe the police would grab onto it.

Holly sighed impatiently and tapped a pile of papers
against her desk. "I really am kind of busy here."

"A girl's got to eat. Come on, what do you say?" So, she
didn't know.

"I have plans."

"Plans?"

"That's right. I'm having lunch with Nick."

A tiny alarm went off in Todd's reptilian brain. "Nick?
Nick who?" He scanned the office for Nicks. Spotted a likely
candidate leaning over the copy machine.

"Your friend, Nick Durham. We're going to go over his
financial picture. See if we can work out a loan for him. Get
him pre-approved."

"You're having lunch with *my* Nick?" What the hell was
going on?

"It's business, Todd. You said yourself he's looking for a place. He called this morning asking what sort of paperwork might be required. I think he's worried how the divorce might affect his credit."

"Right, divorce." Todd's head spun. So, Jolly Ole St. Nick was looking to dump the little woman. Not surprising since Todd was about to dump fifty grand in his lap. But was Durham moving in on his territory? His girl?

Holly scooped up her purse along with the stack of papers. "Call me later, okay? Here's your car keys." She jangled his keyring then let it drop into his open hand. "The car's out back. I'll catch a ride with one of the girls."

Or one of the boys, thought Todd. Like good old Nick.

His fist closed around the keys like a clamshell. Jagged edges dug into his palm. He enjoyed the sharp pain. "Sure, Holly. I'll call you later." Todd bit into his lip, tasted blood. He watched her go.

The cellphone in his jacket rang as he headed back to his office, top down, letting the sun burn away his worries and his cares. He'd arrange for the dealer to pick up the BMW at Sunshine. Had to get the mangled front end repaired anyway and the convertible was a nice change of pace. "Y'ello?"

It was Caroline. And she was sobbing.

:20

There was an Aventura police cruiser in the driveway and a black four-door sedan angled at the curb when Todd arrived.

Caroline answered the door herself. Todd bristled seeing the uniformed cops sitting on her sofa and the blue-suited and authoritative gentleman with the hook nose and thick gray hair seated across from them. They reeked of officialdom.

Caroline's arms went around Todd's neck. She smelled of fine French perfume. He knew Caroline ordered the stuff custom-blended from Paris. She wore a plain but expensive looking black dress and heels. One carat princess cut diamond earrings glittered on each slightly detached lobe. "Thank you for coming."

Todd nodded, casting a questioning glance at the visitors in the living room.

She pulled him inside. "Let me introduce you. Todd, this is Capt. Johnson from the Coast Guard and these are officers Hopkinson and Lao-Yin." Clutching Todd's hand, she pulled him down onto the oversized leather chair near the fireplace. "This is Todd Jones. A dear friend of Doug's." She patted his hand. "A dear friend to both of us."

Todd said hello. The chair felt like a witness stand and he felt all too guilty. But that was nonsense. What did he have to feel guilty about? What did he have to worry about? He forced a smile, lots of teeth. Sell yourself, Todd. Sell yourself.

They asked a lot of routine questions. What was the state of the doctor's mind? How long had he been boating? How knowledgeable was he of boating safety? When was the last time either of them had seen or heard from him?

"I don't understand. I'm in shock," said Todd. "I saw Doug just Friday afternoon for my checkup. He seemed a little rundown maybe, but fine otherwise." Thinking this might be a good time to try out the suicide angle again, Todd said, "He could have been depressed. Caroline?"

Caroline looked confused. "I-I don't know. My husband wasn't the happiest guy in town, but I don't know if I'd call him depressed." She smiled. "He hadn't been too happy with the stock market. That's for sure."

Officer Lao-Yin said, "Who has? My wife used to do some daytrading." He shook his head. "No more. Lost it all and then some."

Rather routine and mundane questioning continued, then trailed off. Soon they were gone. Capt. Johnson promised he'd contact Caroline as soon as Doug's body was recovered. She thanked him.

Todd handed Caroline a martini. "What was that all about?"

She sunk into the sofa and sipped her drink. "Just routine.

Paying their condolences, dotting all the I's, crossing all the T's." She patted the cushion next to her. "Can you stay? Keep me company?"

"Caroline. . .I can't."

"What is it? Now that Doug's gone, I'm no longer attractive to you?"

He set down his empty glass. "Of course you are. I've got some business I have to take care of. That's all. And I promised Holly I'd call her."

"That's perfect."

"What?"

"I asked Holly to come over. I called her after speaking with you. She was with a client, but she said she'd come by for dinner."

Todd crossed the room, his face contorted in disbelief. "You asked her to come here?"

Caroline smiled. "Sure. Why not?"

"Why not?" Todd pulled his hair. "What if she finds out about us?"

Caroline rose and wrapped a hand around Todd's waist. "Relax, baby. She's not going to find out. The only people that could tell her are you and I. I'm not about to tell her. Are you?"

Todd caught a deep breath. "No."

She leaned up and kissed him. He kissed her back.

His cellphone rang and he answered it.

"You didn't tell me it was a freakin' ocean. You don't need fill, you need a freakin' volcano to lift Florida up a good ten inches."

Todd shouted into the phone. "Who is this?"

125

"Jack. Jack Custer."

Jack Custer? Who the hell was Jack Custer?

"You better meet me. You can't just go dumping a truck full of fill out here. You're going to need permits and some sort of buttressing, maybe some gravel for a foundation."

Todd rubbed his eyes. Jack Custer. The guy with the clean fill. "Fine. Whatever. Now is not a good time, Jack. Can we talk about this later."

"It's your call, Mr. Jones. But this is a big project. Gonna take time—and money. I thought you were in a hurry?"

Todd sighed. He pulled himself free of Caroline and paced to the pool deck. "I am in a hurry, Jack. But I'm sort of in the middle of something."

"That's cool. I'm going to be out of town until the end of next week, going to see the wife's family up in Jersey, but you give me a call sometime next week when I get back and we'll—"

"Next week! That won't do." He couldn't put off Constantine that long. He needed answers quick. Todd looked at Caroline. She wanted him to stay. A part of him wanted to stay. A certain neglected part.

"You there?"

"Yes. I'm thinking. Listen," said Todd, "how about if I meet you up at the lots." Todd studied his watch and picked a time. Jack agreed to meet him in about an hour and a half.

Caroline was leaning against the open slider.

"I don't have much time."

She grinned seductively. "I don't need much time."

:21

By the time Todd extricated himself from Doug's horny bereaved widow, it was nearly time for his appointment with Jack Custer. Custer was waiting in his Ford Explorer jotting columns of figures on a yellow legal pad. Todd tapped on his window. A cloud of cigar smoke escaped and Todd coughed.

"Jack Custer?"

The fellow spit out the nub of his cigar. "S'right. You Mr. Jones?" He held out a warm, damp and jaundiced hand. Todd shook it with reluctance. "This is one hell of a job you've got here."

"Tell me about it." Todd stepped aside as Custer clambered out of his vehicle and started waving his pencil out over the water.

The guy was spouting some gobbledy-gook about cubic feet of fill and yards of gravel, concrete pilings, EPA approvals and material mass-density options. Todd cut him off with a wave of his hand. "Let's cut to the bottom line."

Custer crossed his arms over his chest and thrust his hands under his armpits. "Okay." His jaw worked back and forth for a moment. "All this swamp yours?"

"From house to house, excepting about a ten foot setback on each side. And you've got the depths of the lots on the sheet."

Custer turned the sheet over and laid it over the hood of his Explorer. The pencil went to work. He held the paper in front of Todd's nose and tapped it with the eraser end of the pencil. "This is what you're going to need." The pencil bounced off a big number then fell lower. "And this is how much it's gonna cost you." This number was even bigger.

Todd whistled.

"Maybe you want to just forget about this, Mr. Jones."

Todd shook his head. "I can't. It's not even an option." He grabbed the sheet from Custer's fingers. "Isn't there some way you can massage these numbers?"

"Nope. Maybe you want to get another estimate? Find somebody cheaper?"

Todd pushed his fingers into his temples. He didn't have time for this shit. This was supposed to be a good day. His troubles scattered to the Seven Seas. "No," he said finally. "Let's do it."

Custer nodded. "When you want to get started?"

"You said we need permits?"

"Definitely."

"We'll get started on that. I have to talk to the actual developer. I'm only his agent. Put this all in writing and fax me your quote. I'll get the developer to sign off on it and we'll get moving."

Custer agreed and drove off.

Surfer Steve was standing in the wake of the Explorer as

it disappeared around the bend. "What's up, bro' ?" He had on a pair of oversized surfer shorts, yellow background, red poppies and a white T-shirt advertising Baccardi.

Todd shrugged. "Taking care of a little leg work. I see you came back home."

"Yeah, it's cool."

"Your father isn't pissed?"

Steve smiled. "Nah. Said it's no worse than the shit he did when he was a kid."

Todd rolled his eyes. With the sunglasses on, Steve never noticed. What a family this kid was part of that bullet holes and drug deals were considered the harmless escapades of youthful zest?

"My old man wants to talk to you." Steve nodded towards the manse.

"Oh?" Todd smiled. Maybe he'd get a new listing out of his association with the kid. That just might make everything he'd gone through because of Steve—from being shot at by punks to almost having his knees busted by Thug Peter— worth the while.

Todd followed Steve across the street. The house had to be ten or eleven thousand feet under air and worth at least five mil. Even if Todd only pocketed the listing money, he'd be up one hundred and fifty grand.

Steve led him into the study, a mahogany lined, coffered ceilinged room the size of a modest house. Three tall glass gun cases drew Todd's eyes. Polished weaponry of all sizes and manner filled them. He steadied his nerves. Nothing unusual about this. Steve had said his dad was a gun manufacturer or dealer. Some such thing.

Speaking of which, an elegantly dressed man, nearly six and a half feet tall, rose from a leather desk chair and introduced himself. "Yevgeny Brezhinski."

Todd gave his name. "A pleasure to meet you, sir." Todd sized up his new client. A refined man with manicured fingernails and clipped gray hair. His weather-lined face was richly tanned. He was dressed casually, though, in Tommy Bahamas silk shorts and shirt. Tasseled leather loafers on his feet.

A small red blemish under Brezhinski's left eye gave the appearance of a permanently tattooed red tear drop. Like he was crying blood. When Brezhinski showed his teeth, he looked both happy and sad all at once.

"I hear you are responsible for building across the street."

"Yes, sir. That is, I'm the agent for the builder. They'll be estate size homes, of course. Perfect for the neighborhood. You won't have to worry about that. No, sir."

Mr. Brezhinski pointed to a chair. Todd sat and Brezhinski returned to his own seat behind the desk. His elbows rested on the desktop, his chin rested on his hands. "You have permission from the city for this?"

"Yes, sir, Mr. Brezhinski. Last four developable lots on the Intracoastal in Boca," Todd said proudly.

Brezhinski's wide eyelids fluttered. "It's going to spoil the view of the water."

Todd squirmed. "Is that why you've decided to sell?"

Brezhinski's lips tightened into a smile. "Selling? I am not selling, Mr. Jones. I am buying."

Todd shot a look at Surfer Steve who shrugged uselessly. "Buying, Mr. Brezhinski?"

The old man leaned forward. "I want you to sell me the property across the street." His smiled hardened. So did his dark brown eyes. "I do not wish my view spoiled."

Todd gulped. "Sell *you* the property?"

That was impossible. He didn't even own it. Maybe he could convince Constantine to give up one of the lots. He'd still be able to build on the other three. And Constantine wouldn't have to spend money filling in the empty lot across from Brezhinski either. That was it. That was the angle he'd use. He'd explain to Constantine how he could save money by selling an undeveloped lot to Brezhinski.

Brezhinski didn't look like the unreasonable type. Surely he'd be willing to let Constantine make a profit on the deal?

"You mean the lot across from your house?"

"I mean all of it."

"But, Mr. Brezhinski—"

The old man held up his hand. "I'm not an unreasonable man, Mr. Jones. I will pay above their assessed value. What did your client pay for the property?"

"Four million. A million bucks a lot."

Brezhinski nodded. "I see. I will pay you six." He came to his feet. "A very nice profit for your client. Don't you agree?"

Todd stood. He was being dismissed.

Brezhinski walked him to the study door. Steve was right behind. "I'll take care of you, too, Mr. Jones. I'll pay you a five percent commission on the deal, on top of what I am willing to pay for the property. That's a three hundred thousand dollar profit."

The old man patted Todd on the shoulder. "Draw up the papers and you'll be a rich man, Mr. Jones." He turned to his son. "Please see Mr. Jones out, Steve."

The old man hadn't even asked if they had a deal. He was expecting to get his way. What would happen if he didn't?

:22

"Dude, are you lucky or what?" Steve slapped Todd across the back, sending him over the edge of the front porch and into the Mexican heather.

"Yeah," said Todd, dusting himself off and readjusting his tie. "Mr. Lucky, that's me."

"Yeah. You're gonna make a bundle. Sure wish my old man would throw some of his money my way once in a while. Hey, come on," said Steve heading towards the garage, "I want to show you something."

Todd sighed and followed along. All he really wanted to do was get home. No, scratch that. His mother would be waiting for him there. Christ, was there no place he could be alone? The office? No, some of his realtors burned the midnight sales oil.

Maybe he'd call Holly and see what happened with Durham. No, scratch that, too. Holly was probably with Caroline now.

Todd shivered at the thought of what they might find to talk about. What did the two ladies have in common besides him? He looked at his watch. He'd cut out of here as quick as possible and hustle on down to Aventura before Caroline spilled her guts about their relationship.

Steve punched some buttons on a keypad attached to the garage. Todd was impressed. The garage held six immaculate vehicles. The chill air confirmed his suspicion that the garage was climate controlled. Imported Italian tile lined the floor. Oak paneling covered the walls. Probably cost more to decorate this garage than it had his condo. There was original art on the walls.

The cars were all beauties, too. A Rolls, a Mercedes, Hummer, BMW, one of those new VW Bugs and a shimmering dark Porsche. Steve ran his hand lovingly along the edge of the German masterpiece. "It's the new GT2. Saw it in the showroom when we took the Boxster down for repairs. The guy who'd ordered it was unable to take delivery. Dad snatched it up. Said I could drive her until I get my own wheels back."

Todd nodded appreciatively. Black paint and black leather interior. Six speed. He inhaled the heady aroma of new car. Top of the line new car. No scent could compare to that.

"Cost him one hundred ninety-grand," Surfer Steve said rather proudly.

"Nice." Todd stuck his head in the open passenger side window. Very nice.

"Want to drive it?"

"What?"

"I said do you want to drive it?"

The hair on the back of Todd's neck bristled. He shook his head. "No, I shouldn't."

Steve smiled. "Come on, bro'. It's cool."

"No," Todd replied. "I have an appointment down in Aventura. A dinner, actually."

Steve shrugged. "So, take the GT. Get her out on the highway. See how she handles. Had her up to one-fifty myself this afternoon."

Todd nodded towards the street. "I've already got a car."

Steve squinted towards the Sebring. "Tell you what. You take the GT and I'll follow you down in your car. That way you get to test the Porsche and we'll swap them out when we get there."

Todd reached over and massaged the steering wheel. He'd always wanted to try one of these babies but had never had the chance. Besides, he'd never been able to afford one before and hadn't wanted to make himself sick with longing when he test drove one and discovered how much he loved it. It was a bear going back once a person got used to the finer things that life had to offer.

Of course, the way things were going, he just might be able to order up one of these cars himself. Or perhaps a Turbo. They were a bit cheaper. A bright red one with black leather and lots of polished aluminum inside like this one.

"Go for it, dude." Steve's voice was slicker than an oil spill. "I'm heading in that direction, anyway. Got a date in Miami."

"I don't know. . ."

A leather pouch dropped into view. "Here's the key," said Steve.

Todd took it.

The kid was right. Sitting behind the wheel, foot on the gas, it was like a dream. The Porsche was everything he'd thought it would be and more. He imagined everyone he passed looking at him with envy; envy and longing.

Todd's grin was as wide as the front seat. In a clear stretch, he pushed the speedometer up to one twenty-five. He stole a look in the rearview mirror to see how Steve was keeping up in the rented Sebring. There was no sign of the kid. Todd slowed down to ninety, then eighty.

Still no sign of the Sebring. He cut over to the center lane and slowed to seventy. Where the hell was Steve? He lifted his foot further and further until the driver behind leaned on his horn. Todd pulled over to the side of the highway, flashers flashing.

He looked at his watch, waited five minutes. "Sonofabitch." Todd squeezed the gearshift with all his might. "Where the hell are you, Steve?"

A Florida Highway Patrolman pulled up behind and asked Todd if everything was all right. Todd said it was, that he was only checking his map.

Todd breathed more easily after the officer was gone. At least he hadn't asked him for his license or, worse yet, the registration.

He carefully headed on to Caroline's house, keeping an eye open for Steve and/or his Sebring. Neither appeared. And the cop hadn't noticed that Todd had no map and that the Porsche was equipped with GPS.

As he approached the front door, it opened and Holly stepped outside. "Todd, here you are. Caroline said you might be coming."

Todd nodded. "Sorry I'm late. Had some troubles."

Holly walked all around the GT2. "New car? Very nice. I didn't know business was that good."

"It's not." He explained how he'd borrowed it from a client.

"Nice client," replied Holly. "Give him my card. Maybe he needs some banking."

"I will." He laced his arm through Holly's. "Shouldn't we be getting inside?"

Holly shook her head. "I've put Caroline to bed."

"Kind of early, isn't it?"

"She's had a tough day. A long day. I think the tragedy is only now beginning to strike her. Barely touched her dinner. Drank too much."

"You think she's awake?"

Holly shrugged. "Maybe. Why?"

"Thought I'd go say goodnight." Todd started for the door. "You coming?"

"No, it's been a long day for me, too. Think I'll go."

Todd hurried back to her. "No, wait. Don't go. I wanted to talk to you."

She waited, her foot lightly tapping the pavers.

"How did your lunch with Durham go?"

"Good. I don't think he'll have any trouble getting approved as long as he comes with the cash down that he says he's got. Even with the divorce and the house he's in now being in his wife's name."

"I'm sure he will if he says he will."

"I guess." She was curling a lock of hair around her finger. "It's a lot of cash though. Wouldn't think he'd have that much, being a policeman."

"Maybe he's a good saver or came into it. A rich aunt."

"Could be. In any case, with a one hundred thousand dollar down payment I could get a homeless, and out of work telecom exec approved."

"One hundred—" Sonofabitch. Todd had only promised Durham fifty. And the house in Plantation belonged to the wife. Where was the other fifty coming from? The bastard wasn't thinking of squeezing him, was he?

"Something wrong?"

"No. Let me go say goodnight to Caroline. We'll go have a drink after."

"I have to work tomorrow."

"Me, too. We'll keep it short."

"I don't know. . ."

"I'll follow you up to your place and then we'll take the Porsche. I've got it for the night."

Holly agreed and drove off.

Todd entered the house. The front door was unlocked. "Caroline?"

A light shone from the downstairs master bedroom. He knocked lightly on one of the double doors with his knuckles, heard no response and entered. A lone bedside lamp lit a corner of the room near the bed. Caroline was lying in her bed, the covers pulled up to her waist. She wore a sheer black negligee. She looked cold.

Her eyes opened as he neared the bed. "Hello there. Didn't hear you come in."

"You must have dozed off."

Caroline nodded and rubbed her cheeks. "Come to keep

me company?"

"Sorry I missed dinner." She patted the bed and he sat on the edge. "So, what did you girls talk about?"

"Oh, I told her how I was fucking her boyfriend and how good he was in bed."

Todd jumped to his feet.

She laughed. "Relax. What do you think?"

Todd sat back down.

"We talked about Doug, silly. Going to be strange not having him around."

Todd nodded. "Yeah."

"Take off your clothes," Caroline said. "Keep me warm."

"I can't. Holly's waiting for me."

Caroline leaned forward, kissed him and pushed his hand to a barely concealed breast. "Too bad. Maybe I should call Holly back and really tell her about you. I'll bet she'd be fascinated with what I could tell her."

Todd frowned. His hand stiffened.

"Ouch." Caroline pushed his hand away. "Better still, maybe I should tell the police how you murdered my husband."

Todd turned away with a laugh. "That's ridiculous." She couldn't possibly know, could she?

"Is it? You say Doug was trying to kill you and the next thing I know, Doug is dead."

Todd heard the rustle of the silk sheets and turned. Caroline had flung her legs over the side of the bed. She rubbed her thighs tauntingly.

"I wonder what the police would think," Caroline said, "if they knew that you and Doug were having a problem. If they knew you were sleeping with me."

Todd stood over her. "You'd never do that. You'd never tell the police any of that."

"Why not? I didn't kill anyone. I've got nothing to hide." She spread her legs ever so slightly. "Nothing."

Todd rubbed his thumbs together. "What is it you want?"

She made him promise to come back later. He agreed. "Lock up on your way out, would you, Todd? There's a key on the table near the door. Take it."

Todd retreated, found the key where Caroline said it would be and left.

He took Holly to one of his favorite nightspots, a popular restaurant on the Intracoastal Waterway in Ft. Lauderdale where the boaters hung out. Over drinks, he convinced her to take a few days off and go to the Bahamas with him. "We'll take the Searay," he said. "I really could use a vacation. I'll bet you could, too."

"What about your Mother?" Todd had explained how she was staying with him for a few days.

"She'll be fine. I'll give her a credit card. She'll do some shopping, clean out the Bal Harbour Shops." Bal Harbour was a shopping mecca of international renown down on Collins Avenue in Bal Harbour. Once the site of an army barracks, the small upscale mall housed many of the world's elite brands.

"What about Doug's funeral?"

"The police don't even have a body yet," replied Todd. "How can there be a funeral?"

In the end, Holly agreed. They'd pack in the morning and

be out by afternoon.

At her door, Holly invited Todd inside. "Spend the night?"

"I'd better not. You know, Mom and all." He kissed her forehead. "I'll see you tomorrow though and we'll have the whole long weekend together."

It was nearing midnight when he arrived back at Port Lauderdale. It hadn't been easy getting Caroline to let him go. She was going to be trouble. He could see that now. He'd have to do something about her.

Todd tiptoed through his apartment, feasting on the view of stars from his window. He pictured God walking around with a pocketful of diamonds. This was what it would look like from inside that big, soft pocket.

His mother's room was dark and quiet. Good.

It was amazing how the whole apartment stank of nicotine and White Shoulders after so short a time. But he didn't let it get under his skin.

Things were back on track. The day hadn't been as bad as it might have become. For a moment there, it looked like his life might be spinning out of control again, like a planet knocked out of orbit by a giant, rogue asteroid. But once again, he had overcome all obstacles.

And tomorrow he'd leave for the Bahamas with Holly. A few days of fun and sun, that was precisely what the doctor ordered. No Aristotle Constantine, now Yevgeny Brezhinski, no Thug Peter, no Surfer Steve, no Intracoastal swamps, no Det. Durham or on-the-brink of bankruptcy Kendall Kastles, no Jack 'clean fill' Custer and no ball-breaking Caroline Freeman.

Todd grinned.

Best of all: No Doug Freeman.

Todd poured himself a nightcap and climbed into bed. As for the GT2, if he didn't hear from Steve, he'd leave it downstairs with Carlos and Steve could come and get it when he was good and ready. As for the Sebring—it was a rental. No big loss.

Todd shut his eyes, ice cube chilled glass clutched in his hand. He pictured a long stretch of pristine white beach and Holly in a bikini. A few days on the beach and he was sure he could figure out some way out of his troubles over those damn lots up in Boca. Get Constantine and Brezhinski off his back.

And get rich in the process.

He'd have to find something or somebody to distract Caroline, too. He meant what he'd decided earlier. He was going to be a one woman man. Maybe he'd even ask Holly to marry him.

Well, some day.

:23

"I hear you're getting yourself pre-approved for a home loan." Todd very purposefully hoisted his paper cup and took a tentative sip of lip-burning coffee.

Nonchalant. Look nonchalant. Act nonchalant. Like you just don't give a rat's ass.

He inhaled. The enervating scent of freshly ground coffee beans sent signals of joy and happiness through his jangled nerves. A piece of dark Swiss chocolate would go perfectly right about now. Or a beignet, like the ones at Café du Monde up in New Orleans. God, they were great.

"That's right," said Durham, dumping some artificial creamer into his own cup and pushing it around. "Thought I'd try, at least. Thought I might try living on my own again."

The men were meeting at a small coffee and bagel place around the corner from the main branch of the Broward County Library.

Todd nodded. "That's nice." He kept his voice low, calm and under control. "A hundred thou. That's a lot of money. You ought to get someplace decent with a down payment like

143

that."

"Hope so." Durham paused and chewed off the end of his toasted sesame seed bagel. "Nothing so nice as your place, of course. But I hope I can find someplace decent. Maybe something on a little canal somewheres."

The detective's eyes looked merrily at Todd. "Maybe get myself a little boat."

"Right." Todd turned and watched a man on a bicycle as he pulled up, rolled down his trousers and ordered a coffee. "Yep. A hundred thousand dollars is a lot of money." His nostrils twitched. "Where do you plan on getting it?"

Durham chuckled softly and pulled apart his bagel with his fingers. "Why, from you, of course." He stuffed a chunk of shredded bagel into his mouth and chomped down on it.

Todd leaned across the tiny table, bumping his legs on the underside and spilling coffee over the top. "That was not our deal."

"I know."

"The deal was fifty." Todd fought to keep his voice under control.

"I know that, too. But the deal's changed."

Todd fell back in his chair and crossed his arms. "I don't think so."

Durham spoke, his mouth full of dough. "I don't think you've got much choice, Todd." He tipped his cup and drank. "Do you?"

"It isn't fair." The sonofabitch. Todd was going to kill him.

"Fair?" Durham snorted. "What are you, in kindergarten?"

"I don't have that kind of cash. And even if I did, how do I know this is going to be the end of it?"

"You mean the word of an officer of the law isn't good enough for you, Todd?"

Durham was smirking. Todd didn't like it. What had he gotten himself into? "I want some insurance."

"What did you have in mind?"

Todd rubbed his nose. "Something in writing. We'll put something in writing saying that I'm paying you one hundred thousand dollars and what you've done to earn it. You sign it, you get your money."

The detective thought this over. "Deal."

"You're going to have to give me some time, though. I'm working on a couple of big deals right now that are going to pay off big."

"I'm a patient guy, Todd."

Todd told Durham to go fuck himself and left.

"I tried telephoning Caroline this morning," Holly said, carrying her makeup kit down into the master bedroom. "But there was no answer."

Todd tossed some fresh fruit and champagne into the small galley refrigerator. "Probably sleeping in. Or doesn't feel like answering the phone."

Holly popped out of the bedroom and threw her arms around Todd's waist. "I still feel guilty leaving her alone at a time like this."

Todd kissed Holly on the mouth. "She'll be fine. In fact, she told me she wanted some time to herself." He patted Holly's behind. "Let's shove off. I'm anxious to get out to sea." He climbed to the bridge and started up the engines. He could see his mother hanging over the railing of the guestroom far above them. He smiled and waved.

She hadn't minded his taking off for a few days at all. In fact, she said it was about time. His mother always accused him of working too hard.

Holly waved, too.

Todd pulled away from the dock with a toot of the horn. "Mom really likes you."

Holly snuggled against Todd. "She's a dear. Though she really ought to give up smoking."

"Never happen. She'll probably insist on having a pack stashed in her coffin. A pack of smokes and a box of matches." And a bottle of White Shoulders.

The ocean breeze greeted him and he welcomed it. The wheels of his problems turned in his mind. Already the trip was paying off. He'd had a good idea, albeit a crazy one.

But wouldn't it be great if he could get Surfer Steve or one of his druggie pals to bump off Not-So-Jolly-Ole Nick? Cops were always getting killed. Maybe rig up a drug deal gone bad.

Speaking of Steve, the two hundred thousand dollar GT2 was parked outside his condo building waiting for the goof's eventual return. Too bad Todd couldn't sell the car on the black market and pay the crummy detective off with the proceeds. He'd be nothing out of pocket that way. Maybe even clear a few bucks for himself.

If Stevie-boy hadn't come back for it by the time Todd returned from the Bahamas, he just might do that. Hell, he'd say the car had been stolen.

Wouldn't be his fault.

"Not a chance of us blowing up, is there?" asked Holly.

"Not a chance," said Todd. "This boat runs on diesel. Doug made the mistake of using gasoline." Dougie-boy had made too many mistakes, like trying to kill him. "Very flammable stuff, gasoline is." Life was full of winners and losers. Doug was a loser.

The boat got into Nassau ahead of schedule, where they checked in with the harbormaster and had lunch at one of the big resorts. Holly wanted to stroll around town afterwards and Todd let her have her way.

They went to the Straw Market where Holly purchased some native Taino crafts, a necklace and a hammock; souvenirs for her sister and her dad respectively. She also picked up a set of four woven placemats in the shapes of fish for herself.

Holly's sister and dad shared a small house in Ft. Lauderdale not far from Holly's place. Todd thought the old man was pretty cool, but the sister was a bit of a pain. And she didn't like Todd. That was probably the reason he didn't like her.

Her father, Charles, had been a programmer with IBM and taken early retirement when the company closed up most of its Boca offices and moved north to North Carolina. Charles spent his mornings surfing the waves and his afternoons surfing the web. Maybe Charles and Surfer Steve should hook up. Holly's mother had died years ago, victim of a teenage drunk driver. Todd didn't know much of the story. Holly didn't like to talk about it.

Todd and Holly spent the next couple hours frying in the sun. Holly decided she'd had enough and they returned to the Searay. Todd took a quick shower and changed into a pair of shorts and a loud rayon shirt. "Think I'll pop into town and pick up some fresh fruit. Maybe a couple bottles of champagne. Want to come?"

Holly had her nose in a medical thriller and was stretched out on the bed. "No, thanks. Think I'll relax."

"Suit yourself. Back soon." Todd slipped into his topsiders and went ashore. 'No thanks' was just the answer he'd been looking for. This would give him a chance to get to the bank. He kept a private little pile of cash in a safe deposit box at the Island International Bank and liked to check on it from time to time.

Made him all warm and fuzzy to look at his quarter million and change, to breathe in its heady, musky aroma.

He stopped at a small market, picked up two bottles of Moet and Chandon, some salmon steaks and asparagus. The bank was just around the corner and it was nearly closing time. He showed his ID and hurried to open his safe deposit box. He ran his fingers through the cash.

Todd decided to take all of it with him. He might need it to cover some investment loans coming due. If not, he could always put the money back on his next trip. Besides, that sonofabitch Durham was going to take nearly half of it the way things were going. Maybe he really would get Steve or his friends to bump the cop off, he thought, as he busily dumped the contents of his box into his shopping bag, hiding the stacks of bills beneath the steaks. He'd conceal it on the boat until he got back to Fort Lauderdale.

Keeping his bag close to his chest, he hurried along the street. He spotted some guy in a Yankees ballcap and wraparound sunglasses, sporting one fat, ugly moustache, across the street walking in the same direction. He'd noticed the guy earlier as well. Where was it? The Straw Market? The goof looked familiar somehow. Something about that bowlegged stance of his.

Todd glanced at his watch and pressed on. Holly might begin to wonder what was taking him so long. And he didn't want her asking questions. He turned onto a little sidestreet, a shortcut to the dock. A crowd of children in blue and red uniforms squeezed past, giggling.

Todd felt himself being slammed up against the rough brick wall of a shut up dry goods shop. It was the man in the Yankees cap. A knife flashed and raced past Todd's eyes, nicking his nose. Todd swung the bag against his assailant.

A voice cried out from an upstairs window across the narrow street. "Hey, what's going on out there?" Todd glanced up at a white-haired woman with a hooked nose. "I'm calling the police!"

The stranger kicked Todd savagely between the knees and he went down gasping. His chin hit the pavement. He felt himself losing consciousness.

When he opened his eyes, the hook-nose lady was looking at him.

"You okay?"

Todd struggled to his knees and sat against the wall, breathing hard. "Yeah. Okay." He wiped blood from his face. His groin ached liked he'd been kicked by a bull elephant with a grudge.

"I called the police," said the woman, wiping her hands on her apron. "Don't worry. They come."

"Police?" That was the last thing Todd wanted. He pushed himself up, his head spun. Then he remembered his grocery bag. "My money!" He checked the ground. Several stalks of asparagus had spilled over the sidewalk and into the street and lay there crushed. A broken bottle of champagne created an ever changing pattern of dark glass shards and yellow-gold bubbles. "My bag." He grabbed her shoulders and shook. "Have you seen it?"

"Bag?" She pulled away. "What are you talking about, mister? You sit," she said. "Wait for the policeman."

"I had a bag. The mugger must have took it. You must have seen it."

"I didn't see a bag."

Todd moaned. "The man who hit me," he said, "which way did he go?"

The old woman looked confused a moment then pointed in the direction of the water.

Todd hurried away, ignoring her protests to stay put. He ran all the way to the street along the dock and paused there, eyes scanning the milling crowd. Looking for a stinking Yankees cap. A glimpse of blue ahead caught his eye and he raced after it only to discover it was a PGA Tour cap on the head of a guy old enough to play on the Champions Tour, in the Super Senior Division no less. His attacker had been far younger.

And, oddly, Todd thought, from the blur that he'd seen, the mugger looked a bit like Dr. Doug Freeman. But that was impossible. Todd knew Doug was dead.

It was a coincidence, that was all. Either that or Doug's death was beginning to rattle him and he was starting to imagine Doug was out there, like a specter, following him around.

Todd walked slowly to his boat, *Get Real*. His steps were heavy. A quarter of a million dollars. Gone. And he couldn't report it. Couldn't tell a soul.

:24

"Todd, what happened?" Holly leapt from the bed. Her hand went to his face. She gingerly touched his nose.

"I was mugged on the way home."

"Poor baby. Come here," she said, leading him to the sink. "Let's get you cleaned up."

Todd explained how he'd been attacked and the groceries taken. He left out the most important part, the bit about the cash. Holly knew nothing about that and wasn't going to. "The weirdest thing is," said Todd, "that the attacker looked a lot like Doug."

"That's silly," said Holly, wiping his face with a damp cloth. "You're under a lot of stress. You're hallucinating."

Todd winced as she cleaned up his wounds. "Yeah. You're right. Stress. It's a killer. And this was supposed to be a vacation."

"And it's going to be," said Holly, helping him out of his torn shirt. "Take a shower. We're going out to dinner."

"I don't know if I'm up for it," said Todd. "All I feel like doing is crashing."

"Nonsense," said Holly. "What you need is to forget everything bad that's happened and have some fun. Play your cards right and I'll even let you have your way with me, sailor." Her hand played across his chest.

Todd faked a grin because truth be told he wasn't sure if his equipment was up to the task after that vicious kick to his center of gravity.

They dined at a beautiful waterfront restaurant called Shifty's. The lobster was succulent and buttery. The champagne was eighty bucks a bottle but Holly had insisted on it and so they drank. A small, round, mango scented candle flickered between them.

"I have to admit," said Todd, settling back in his upholstered chair and enjoying the view, "I do feel better." He breathed in the salty, humid Caribbean air and yawned luxuriantly.

"I knew you would." She tipped her glass. "I'm always right. Face it, I know what's best for you, Todd."

He grinned. "Maybe you do." God, how he wished he could tell her his troubles. It would be great to have someone to confide in. Maybe if they were married he'd be able to share aspects of his life that for now had to remain hidden.

"What are you thinking?"

"I'm thinking how lovely you look." And she did. Holly had herself all slinked up in a short, tight fitting rose-colored silk dress revealing an elegant rise and fall of cleavage, not too flashy, not too dull. He felt a stirring between his legs. Maybe the old soldier hadn't been mortally wounded after all. "There!"

153

"What?"

"There. Look." Todd pointed towards the bar. "Did you see him?"

Holly looked away and then back at Todd. "See who?"

"Doug."

"Todd," said Holly. "Are you sure you're okay?"

"I'm fine," he complained. "Doug Freeman was standing right there at the bar. Dark brown shorts, white shirt. He waved at me." Todd waved his hand wildly in the air. "Didn't you see him?"

"Todd, baby—" She reached out across the table. "Doug's dead."

Todd ignored her hand. "I'm not kidding, Hol," he said. "And I'm not crazy. It was Doug." He pushed back his chair and rose.

"What are you doing? Where are you going?"

"He's mocking me, Holly. Don't you get it?" Todd's face had turned a deep purple. "He's tried to kill me, stolen all my money and now he's mocking me."

"Really, Todd, baby—"

"Well, he's not going to get away with it!" Todd twisted between the crowded tables, working his way to the long bar along the back.

"Todd! What are you talking about? Who tried to kill you?" Holly half-rose, bumping the table with her knees, knocking over her water glass, leaving a dark wet blotch on her dress. "What money? Todd, come back!"

Todd leaned heavily over the bar. "Hey, excuse me." The bartender turned. "Did you see a guy standing here a minute ago, dark brown shorts, white shirt, hazelnut eyes."

The bartender shrugged.

"He's got black hair, going bald. He's a doctor."

The bartender mumbled something to a coworker who laughed.

Todd snarled. He scanned the tables. Doug, Doug, where are you Doug? No match. Not even close. He raced to the men's room. Checking every stall.

No Doug.

As he hurried back through the main dining room he saw Holly sitting alone at their table, arms crossed over her chest. She was glaring at him like he was crazy.

She just didn't understand. This was life or death.

He pushed through the door and into the humid night. Which way had Doug gone? And what had Doug done with his quarter million dollars?

On a hunch, Todd went to the big hotel next door. He told the receptionist that he wanted to phone his friend, Doug Freeman. She checked her computer and said there was no Freeman registered. So much for hunches.

Todd went back outside. Only then did he notice the stabbing pains in his chest. Like someone was squeezing his heart with a pair of needlenose pliers. How long had he had the pains? Same damn pain he'd had when Holly had insisted he go to see Dougie-boy. The day all his troubles had started.

Jesus, it seemed like it had been years ago. And yet it had been only a matter of days.

He saw a man looking at a television in the window of an electronics store across the street and stepped into the road. Someone hollered 'look out!' Something hit him in the side of the face and he spun round. A hand yanked him back.

"You okay, mister?" A heavyset, dark-skinned man in a loose fitting T-shirt and jeans was casting him worried looks.

"Yeah," said Todd. He ran a tentative hand along his face. "Yeah. I'm okay."

"That truck almost hit you. Lots of traffic here at night. You better be more careful."

Todd nodded. The man's wife told him to come along and they disappeared. A jolt of pain caused Todd to double over. There at his feet lay a salmon steak. A one hundred dollar bill was pinned to it with a toothpick. He'd had two identical steaks in his grocery bag when he'd been attacked.

It was Doug. It had to be. He pulled out the toothpick and crumpled the bill in his fist.

Doug was alive and he was taunting him.

:25

Todd rolled over. Holly was sleeping. He carefully crawled out of bed. He checked the clock. It was one fifteen a.m. She'd give him hell if he woke her, especially if she knew what he was up to.

He'd had a hard enough time when he'd gone back inside Shifty's. Holly had been pretty steamed. Todd figured it was almost lucky that he'd been mugged earlier in the day. Holly placed the blame for his strange behavior on his being attacked. If not for that, they'd still be duking it out.

Todd crawled around the small, dark room, found his clothes and pulled them on. There was a public phone at the end of the dock.

The phone rang and rang. He almost hung up, but decided to hold on, letting it ring longer and longer. A cry in the night. A nightingale searching for his mate.

"Hello?"

Shit, a woman's voice. It was Durham's wife. He searched his mind quickly. What was her name? Theresa? He gave it a shot. "Hello, Theresa. This is Todd Jones. I know it's late, but is Nick there? Can I speak with him?"

"My name is Trish. Patricia."

"Sorry."

"Who'd you say you are?"

"Todd, Todd—" He heard the distinctive click of someone picking up the other line.

"Hello?" Durham's voice.

"It's me, Todd."

"It's for me, Trish. Go back to bed."

"Who's calling so late at night?"

"Police business."

Todd heard a long suffering sigh, but at least she'd hung up.

"What's up?"

Todd's hand choked the phone, his voice was hard and urgent. "He's here."

"Who?"

"You know who. Our friend. You said you took care of him."

"Impossible."

"I tell you," hissed Todd. "He's here. I've seen him with my own two eyes."

There was a long silence before Durham replied. "It's late. I don't think this is the time to talk about this. Where are you?"

"Nassau."

"The Bahamas?"

"That's right."

The detective asked Todd when he was coming home and told him to give him a call then. "Telephone connections can be unreliable. Know what I mean?"

Suddenly, Todd did. Who knew what ears might be listening in? He'd have to wait until he got back to Florida and could confront Durham in person, in private. He hung up the phone and slunk back to his boat.

Holly woke to the smell of frying eggs and sausage. She rubbed her eyes. "Morning."

"Breakfast in bed, milady." He laid a tray across her lap.

She laced her hands around his neck and planted a lingering kiss on his lips. "Thanks." She sipped her coffee. "What's on the schedule for today?"

He clasped her hand. "We have to go back."

She straightened and the tray tipped. He caught it. "Back where? You mean Fort Lauderdale?"

He nodded. "Something has come up."

"What?"

Todd turned away, thinking of an answer. "Something's come up at the office. Constantine's causing all kinds of havoc."

"But we just got here. I asked for the rest of the week off. The supervisor was all bent out of shape," Holly complained. "You don't know what I went through."

"I'm really sorry, baby. I'll make it up to you."

She pouted. "When are we leaving?"

"We've got plenty of time. Relax, eat your breakfast. I'll prep the boat and we'll be underway."

Todd noticed the Porsche was gone from the visitor's parking space where he'd left it in front of the building.

Good. One less thing to worry about. Except that he still kind of liked that idea about reporting the car stolen and selling it off.

Carlos wasn't around and the guy on duty looked new, at least Todd had never seen him before, so he'd ask about the car later.

Holly asked if she could come up and use his shower and followed him upstairs. She hadn't had time to wash before they'd shipped out. How could he say no?

Todd had had hours to think about his situation and what to do. The first thing was to set up a meeting with Durham and see what had gone wrong. As he and Holly marched up the hallway to his apartment an odd odor filled the air.

"Smells like smoke," said Holly.

"You notice it, too?"

She waved a hand in front of her nose. "Who could miss it?"

Todd stuck his key in the lock and opened the door. The smell of fresh smoke stung his nostrils and eyes. Jesus, how many Camels a day was Mom smoking?

"Whew," said Holly. "What have you been doing in here?"

"I haven't been doing anything." Todd stepped into the kitchen. It was a mess, but nothing was burning. "Weird."

"Uh, Todd."

"What?"

"You'd better come here."

Todd went to the living room. Holly was facing the guestroom.

Or what was left of it.

Todd's mouth fell open. The doorway was a black, smudgy portal, the carpet a damp, ash smeared morass. "What the—" His eyes had gone the size of supernovas. He rushed inside. The room was gutted.

The bed was a tarry, soggy lump. The clock radio on the night table had melted down. The TV on the dresser looked like it had exploded. The once eggshell walls now looked more like the sides of a bombed out crater. The sliding glass doors leading out to the balcony were shattered and sheets of plastic clung to the opening with silver duct tape.

And still he could smell that stinking White Shoulders.

He felt fingers closing around his. "What do you think happened?" asked Holly.

He shook his head.

"I thought I heard voices. You kids are home early."

Todd and Holly turned around. Todd's mother stood in the doorway in a canary yellow housecoat and blue slippers. Her hair was in curlers. There were purple bags under her eyes. A cigarette stuck to her lower lip like an appendage.

"Mom," said Todd. "What happened?"

"Oh, this?" She pulled out her cigarette and tossed it into a puddle on the floor. "Had a little fire."

"A little fire!"

"Are you all right, Mrs. Jones?" Holly had draped an arm over the old woman's shoulders.

Mrs. Jones nodded. "A little shaken. That's all."

"When did this happen?" demanded Todd.

"Yesterday. Last night, actually." She dropped her eyes. "I fell asleep. When I woke up, the place was on fire."

"You poor dear," said Holly.

Todd stomped through the puddles and broken glass, busted knickknacks and charred bits of wood. "You fell asleep smoking and watching television, didn't you, Mother?"

Mrs. Jones looked at Holly.

"Mother—"

"Todd," said Holly, "I don't think you should be talking to your mother this way. She's been through a terrible ordeal. She might have been killed."

"What way?"

"You're yelling at her."

Todd's voice went up thirty decibels. "I am not yelling at her!"

Holly arched her brow at him and he turned away in frustration.

"I'll say one thing," Mrs. Jones began, "you've got one fine fire department in this town." She snapped her fingers. "Why, they got here in nothing flat. A lot faster than they did in my building. Half my building was gone before those jokers even showed up and figured out how to hook up their hoses."

Todd snapped around. "You mean this has happened before?"

"Well. . ." Mrs. Jones took a step back.

Todd's face lit up with enlightenment. "You burned down your condo, didn't you, Mom? That's why you're here. That's why you're visiting me. You burned down your condo and now you've got no place to live."

Mrs. Jones looked once more to Holly for support. "And they kicked me out. Can you believe it? Said I was endangering the lives of the other residents."

Mrs. Jones nervously lit up another cigarette that she'd pulled out of one pocket of her housecoat with a lighter she'd pulled out of the other. "Nonsense. Besides, nobody there's under seventy anyway. How much life do they think any of them got left?"

Todd stormed out and went to his room. Which now appeared to be his mother's room. Her things were scattered everywhere and a cumulonimbus sized cloud of cigarette smoke and White Shoulders seemed to hang over his bed waiting to rain down.

His mother came in, puffing away. "Don't worry, Todd. Insurance will pay."

He forced a smile. "Right, Mom. Where's Holly?"

"She left. Nice girl. Said she'd give you a call later and see if there was anything she could do to help." Mrs. Jones reached up and started unwrapping her curlers. "Oh," she said, "the police came by looking for you."

"What? About the fire?"

"No." Mrs. Jones shook her head and curlers flew in every direction. Ash, too. "No. Fella said some lady by the name of Carol-Caroline Freeman, that was it. Nice fella, too. And the police here have nice uniforms. I like them better than the one's in Naples. Cuter."

"Never mind the uniforms, Mom. What about Caroline Freeman?"

"Man said she was dead."

:26

Todd covered his mouth and stifled a yawn. He was bone tired.

"Am I keeping you awake, Mr. Jones?" The detective tapped the desk with a tightly wrapped manilla folder. The Caroline Freeman case.

"Seems to me there's not much I can tell you. I wasn't even in Florida when Caroline was killed." When Todd had telephoned the Aventura Police Department, he'd learned that Caroline Freeman had been murdered.

"Nasty scratches you've got there."

Todd's hand went instinctively to his face.

"What happened?"

"I was mugged."

Detective Foster nodded. "Lots of crime out there. Better be careful."

Todd pressed his spine against the hardbacked chair. "I am."

"How long were you and Miss Gaines in the Bahamas?"

"Only a day."

"Long way to go for such a short trip."

"Something came up at work."

"What line of work you in?"

"Real estate. You interested in buying?"

The detective wasn't taking the bait. "Let's be frank."

"You be Frank. I'll keep being Todd."

Det. Foster's eyes flattened into gray slabs. "You're a real funny guy. One of Mrs. Freeman's neighbors, a kid coming home late, recognized you leaving the Freeman residence Monday night. Driving a Porsche."

"He could be mistaken."

"No. Don't think so. Said he recognized you as a friend of Mr. Freeman's. Says he's caddied for you out at the country club the Freeman's belong to."

"Okay. So he saw me."

"Want to tell me what you were doing at her house so late?"

Todd twisted in his chair. Why the hell had he ever agreed to come down to the station? The police had no business drawing him into Caroline Freeman's murder. "Not that it's any of your business but I was consoling Caroline."

Det. Foster smiled. "I'll bet."

"Listen, you. I don't like what you're insinuating. Caroline Freeman was as much a friend as Doug was. And, in case you aren't aware, Doug Freeman was supposed to be dead. Caroline was very upset. I was only doing what any friend would do under the circumstances."

Todd wiped his upper lip. A line of perspiration had formed there. Damn the police.

"I see." Det. Foster smoothed out the file folder and

opened it. "Did you know that Mrs. Freeman had had sexual relations within hours of the time she was killed Monday night, early Tuesday morning?"

Todd remained rigid.

"There are tests that can determine who her sex partner was." His eyes locked in on Todd's. "Would you be willing to provide us with a sample so we can rule you out as that partner, Mr. Jones?"

Todd held his breath. His fingers wrapped tightly around the arms of his chair. He watched the second hand of the big clock behind the detective's desk go round and round. He exhaled. "No."

The detective's brow went up.

"I mean, that won't be necessary."

Det. Foster folded his hands, waited.

"Caroline and I did sleep with each other that night. But it was just the one time. She was vulnerable and lonely. We'd had some drinks." Todd used his best closer's smile on the detective. "It was just one of those things. You know how it is."

"Did you file a report?"

"Report?"

"With the police in the Bahamas."

Todd looked confused.

"About that mugging."

Todd's hands went to his face again. "No. It wasn't really a big deal." If you call losing a quarter million dollars to a dead guy that was trying to kill you no big deal. "I decided to forget about it."

"So." Det. Foster locked his hands behind his head. "You

had sex with Caroline Freeman and then?"

"I went home."

"What time was this?"

"I got home around midnight."

"Can anybody verify this?"

Todd sighed. "My mother is staying with me but she was asleep when I got back."

"The doorman at your building doesn't remember you returning."

Todd thought a moment. "I don't remember seeing him either. Hell, maybe he was taking a nap or stealing a smoke out by the Intracoastal. It's not my fault."

A long silence went by and Todd wondered if the detective was finished with him.

"You said something earlier that struck me odd."

"What's that?" Todd scoured his memory. Had he said something stupid? Something that would implicate him in Caroline's death?

"You said that Doug Freeman was supposed to be dead. Mr. Freeman died in a boating accident over the weekend."

Todd leaned over the desk. Should he tell the detective that Doug Freeman was alive and trying to kill him? Or should he wait and discuss it with Durham first?

Damn.

What had he done to be in such an awful position? He decided to chance it. "Listen, detective. I know this sounds crazy, but Doug Freeman isn't dead. He's alive." Todd struggled to keep the hysteria from his voice.

"Dr. Freeman's boat blew up in Coconut Grove. No one could have survived that. Do you have proof?"

"He's the one who mugged me in the Bahamas."

"Did anyone see him?"

"Yes." Todd's fist banged the table. "I mean, no. That is, there was this old woman. She surely saw him. But she wouldn't have known who he was. Try to understand," said Todd, "it's Doug Freeman, don't you see? He killed Caroline. He tried to kill me. And now he's framing me for his wife's murder."

Det. Foster looked far from convinced. Like a million miles far. He stuck his face into Todd's and Todd backed away. "You know what I think, Mr. Jones?"

Todd shook his head.

"I think you were having an affair with Dr. Freeman's wife. I think maybe you got tired of the affair."

"That's not true."

Foster held up his hand. "Or, maybe you and Mrs. Freeman were having an affair and plotted to murder her husband. Husbands can be a complication, can't they?

"Jury's still out on that boating incident. I checked. Maybe the two of you decided to get the good husband out of the picture. Then, you got cold feet. Or maybe there was a falling out between two killers. Maybe she threatened to go to the police and confess what the two of you had done."

"It's not true," repeated Todd, more forcefully.

"So you killed her."

Todd kicked back his chair. "I didn't kill anybody. It's Doug. Doug is trying to kill me!"

Foster looked up at him, appraisingly. "That's quite a temper you've got there, Mr. Jones."

Todd opened his mouth to shout and froze, his fists in

tight balls of rage and impotence against a force that baffled him, baffled him and ensnared him in its malicious web.

He said softly. "I didn't do anything." Todd made a show of looking at his watch. "Can I go now?"

Foster shrugged his shoulders. "Sure. Have a good evening, Mr. Jones."

"Yeah," sneered Todd, turning in the doorway, "I'll do that."

"Oh, Mr. Jones?"

Todd twisted his neck. "Yes?"

"Funny thing."

"Fine. I'll play. What's a funny thing?"

"You never asked *how* Caroline Freeman was murdered."

Shit. "I—" Todd's mind searched for the correct answer. If only the questions were multiple choice, he'd have a fighting chance. "You never gave me a chance. With all your damn questions and accusations." That was a pretty good answer and Todd felt rather proud of himself for thinking so quickly on his rather wobbly feet.

"So?"

Todd knitted his brow. "So what?"

"Don't you want to know?"

Todd's shoulders caved.

"Caroline Freeman was strangled. In her bed. With her nightgown. Traces of semen on that nightgown. You a betting man, Mr. Jones?"

Todd shrugged halfheartedly.

"What do you want to bet that semen is yours?"

:27

"This is all your fault," said Todd. "If you had done your job right, none of this would be happening. I wouldn't be in this position."

"Keep your voice down," said Nick Durham. "You want people to hear? Besides," he said, stepping around the bat exhibit at the Museum of Science and Discovery in downtown Ft. Lauderdale, "I don't know what you're getting all worked up about." A mushy lump of overripe fruit lay in the corner of the exhibit. The bats ignored it.

"You don't know what I'm getting all worked up about? Doug Freeman murdered his wife," Todd whispered harshly. "And he's framed me."

Todd laughed miserably. "The bastard's really fixed me good, too. Everybody thinks he's dead and I get framed for murdering his wife."

"He is dead," said Durham.

"So you claimed. But he isn't."

"He's got to be." Durham followed Todd down the hard, steep steps to the insect exhibit downstairs. A group of kids in matching shirts were squealing at the huge cockroaches.

The two men stood shoulder to shoulder watching a colony of bees, busy at their task. Making the world a sweeter place.

"Say what you want. Doug is alive. He followed me to the Bahamas and tried to kill me." Todd looked around the noisy museum. "He could be in here right now, in the museum, waiting for his chance."

Todd followed after the group of children. He smiled at their harried teacher, a young man in jeans and a matching school T-shirt with a leather pack on his back. "And another thing, Nick," Todd said, "if you think I'm paying you for a botched job, you're crazy."

Durham held Todd's arm and squeezed. "I still say he's dead. But if he is alive, you just show him to me. I'll fix it." He let go of Todd's arm. "And you'll pay me. All of it."

Todd swallowed. "Make sure you do it right this time."

"Leave it to me."

Todd scowled. "I left it to you last time." They rode the escalator up to the space exhibits. "In the meantime, you've got to help me out with the Caroline Freeman investigation."

"Help how?"

"Get the police off my back."

"It's out of my jurisdiction. There's nothing I can do." The detective jumped on a scale displaying his weight on Jupiter, then moved on to Uranus.

"Fine," said Todd, stepping away. "But if the police charge me with murdering Caroline Freeman, all my money is going to be spent on my defense. You'll never see a penny."

"Don't even dream about stiffing me, Todd. I'll rat you

out about the good doctor."

Todd sneered. "Guess what, Nicky, if I'm doing life for strangling Caroline, I'm not going to give a shit what you say or to whom."

Durham gave pause. He rubbed his chin. "I've got some friends. I'll see what I can find out. What I can do."

"You do that." Todd moved away, leaving Durham on Pluto.

Todd drove to his office and studied his phone messages. A number of messages from run-of-the-mill customers. Three from Aristotle Constantine and one from Jack Custer. Another from Steve Brezhinski saying it was urgent. Fat chance he was going to call that jerk back.

Then he remembered, Surfer Steve still had the Sebring. He'd have to get it back. He hoped Steve hadn't run up the mileage.

Finally, there was a message from Tim Tollerton at the rental agency also saying it was urgent that he get in touch with him. An alarm went off in Todd's head. Two plus two suddenly equaled trouble. Had Steve wrecked the Sebring?

He phoned the rental agency and was put through to Tollerton. "Hi, Tim. This is Todd Jones. Got your message. What's up?"

Tollerton went ballistic. "What the hell did you do? What were you thinking?"

"Whoa," said Todd. "What's going on?"

"What's going on is that the police have impounded the car I loaned you. Florida's got these damn seizure laws. Using one of my cars in a drug deal. What you got for brains, shit?"

Todd squeezed his brows together and gritted his teeth. "Slow down. I don't know about any drug deal."

"The car I lent you was abandoned in Little Havana. The police said a suspect was dealing coke and fled. Left the car in the street with the engine running. An eighth of a kilo was found in the glovebox."

"It sure as hell wasn't mine."

"Yeah, well, I'm out a brand new car."

"You must have insurance."

"You think they're going to cover a drug impound?"

"I'm really sorry about that, Tim. I was out of town. I guess somebody took your car. I left it at my building. I thought it would be safe. Somebody must have stolen it."

"You're going to be more than sorry. If you don't reimburse me for the vehicle, my lawyer's going to sue."

Todd asked how much. "Fine," he said. "Fine. I'll pay it. No need to get the lawyers involved." He dropped the phone in the cradle. Sonofabitch. He was going to kill that fucking Steve.

:28

Todd winced.

His hand crept to his spinal column. Since his mother had burned down the guest room and taken over his room, Todd had been relegated to the sofa in the living room. It was meant for sitting, not sleeping, as Todd's aching back constantly reminded him.

The chairs in Athena's were no help, stiff and straight-backed. But Todd wasn't about to complain, not to Aristotle Constantine who owned the small, upscale restaurant near the beach on Palmetto Park Road in Boca Raton.

Todd quietly massaged the muscles along his coccyx as Constantine lashed into him. An image of himself being tied to the mast, his shirt ripped away, while a pirate captain snapped the skin from his back with a long whip came to mind.

"Let me get this straight," said Constantine, between bites of baklava, "you want me to sell one of my lots to some guy so he can *not* build a house on it?"

Todd nodded, nibbling his own Greek dessert. The

baklava was sweet with honey and delicious. This was the real thing, not some Americanized imitation. So good it made his teeth ache.

Todd had already relayed Brezhinski's first offer: to buy all the lots for fifty percent over Constantine's cost. Constantine had shot the idea down like it was nothing more than a WWI Sopwith Triplane up against an F-14 Tomcat. Now he tried again, this time asking for only one. A compromise, he said.

But could he get Brezhinski to agree? Not likely, but he was clutching at straws here and couldn't afford to let any chances slip past.

"One of the four lots under fucking water that you talked me into buying just so I could build houses on them?" Constantine spread his big hands across the linen table cloth.

Thug Peter sat at a separate table near the door reading the Wall Street Journal, sipping a coffee.

"Mr. Brezhinski is willing to pay twice what you've paid." Todd hoped.

"You told me that." Constantine glared. "What you haven't told me is why I should want to do this. I can make ten million dollar houses. You told me this."

This was the hard part, Todd realized. How was he going to justify selling off one lot? He didn't see the sense of it himself, not from Constantine's perspective. If he owned those properties, he'd develop them all, too.

Then again, Brezhinski didn't seem like the kind of guy you wanted to cross. Problem was, neither was Aristotle Constantine.

Todd pushed his hair back over the dome of his skull.

Why did everything have to be so hard? "Maybe I can get Brezhinski to up his offer?" Not impossible, but not likely. Steve's father was already offering an incredibly generous premium for the land.

"Forget it," said Constantine. "We're building houses. Big ones. I saw the copy of the quote you got on getting the dirt and getting the property fit for building."

He shook his head. "The whole thing's a lot of trouble. Lots of engineering. Lots of permits. You didn't tell me this project was going to be so much trouble, Mr. Jones."

Constantine cracked his size thirteen knuckles. "I don't like trouble."

"No, sir."

"But now that we've started, we're going to finish. I've already hired an architect to get to work on plans for the first home. I'm going to put it up on spec. Like I told you before. Like I told your girlfriend."

"What do I tell Mr. Brezhinski?"

Constantine was smiling. "You tell him no. Unless he wants to buy himself a new house. Then you tell him to come see me. Tell him I'll give him a sweet deal." The Greek waved his hand.

Todd scooted back his chair. He'd been dismissed. Was that a look of derision that Thug Peter shot him as he left or was he upset with the financial news?

Todd wouldn't have blamed him if it was derision, about ten thousand shares worth.

A cardboard box was waiting for him outside his condo. He peered over the top. It was all the stuff he'd left at Holly's house. Among the dregs, a silk tie, toothbrush, an old pair of running shoes from that time they'd tried jogging, his Gipsy Kings and Santana CDs.

Shit.

But that was the least of his problems. Tied to the doorhandle by a four foot tether of clothesline was some black, brutish beast with a fuzzy muzzle and eyes like the devil's. Two black stones of death and fury. Short legs, short tail. One fat as hell body.

And it stunk up the hall.

There was a pink envelope tucked under the collar around its neck. The beast snapped at his fingers as Todd pulled it away. He tore open the letter.

Dear Todd,

Spoke with the police. Heard about you and Caroline. Since you're such a pig, I thought I'd get you one to keep you company—since you won't be seeing me any longer.

There was no signature. Gee, guess who.

Todd dug into his pants pocket and retrieved his key. The pig darted inside and screamed when it reached the end of its rope.

"Serves you right," said Todd. He kicked his forlorn looking little cardboard box inside.

"Is that you, Todd, baby? I'm on my way down to the swimming pool. You want to join—" Todd's mother stuck her head out from the bedroom. She was dressed in a skirted one-piece bathing suit the color of a geranium and had one of his good bath towels in her hands. "Oh my, Todd, baby." She came closer. "What have you got there?"

"It's a pig."

"A pot-bellied pig." Mrs. Jones untied the rope from the door handle and the pig took off. He snapped at Todd, turned and leapt onto the sofa. The sofa which was Todd's now temporary sleeping quarters. "Hey!" Todd chased the pig off. He didn't want some smelly pig soiling his bed.

The pig squealed and raced in an ever-widening circle around the living room. Todd got tired of chasing him and left the beast to its own devices.

Mrs. Jones had laid Todd's towel on the ground near the door and set a bowl of water beside it. One of Todd's good bowls. Spode.

"What are you doing, Mother?"

"Making a little bed."

"That was a good towel."

She ignored her son. "I think he's adorable." She clapped her hands and cooed, attempting to draw the filthy beast nearer.

"He's a pig, Mother."

"So?" She rubbed the beast's hairy chin. "Pigs can't be adorable?"

Todd had a very clear opinion on that matter.

"I'm naming him Mr. Squeals. Where on earth did you get him?"

"He was a gift. From Holly."

"How sweet," said Mrs. Jones.

"Yeah, sweet." Todd went to the bar and poured himself a drink. Fortified, he dialed Holly's number. She hung up the moment she heard his voice.

He stepped over Mr. Squeals who was stretched out on his fifty-dollar bath towel in the foyer while his mother fed him scraps of sirloin. "I'm going out, Mother. I'll have to borrow your car again."

He left mother and pig in their own little upside down world. His Mom's bronze Camry was up close in one of Port Everglade's visitor spaces. A shadow passed over as Todd approached the car and he flinched. But it was only a bird. Not a winged Doug Freeman at all.

There was no sign of Doug. Not unless he really was dead and had been reincarnated as pot-bellied Mr. Squeals.

But Todd knew there was no such luck. Doug Freeman was alive and putting the squeeze on him. It had been days. What was Durham doing about it? The detective had warned Todd not to contact him. Too risky, he'd said.

But Todd was tired of waiting and tired of wondering. Waiting and wondering if and when Doug would strike next. Waiting and wondering if and when the police were going to haul him in again, trying to pin Caroline Freeman's murder on him.

Waiting and wondering what Durham was doing to get him out of this jam.

And Holly. A stab of pain went through Todd's chest. This time the pain was emotional. He missed Holly. He missed her a lot.

All this was Doug's fault. Goddamn Doug. If Durham had done his job right, everything would be perfect.

He punched in the detective's number. Durham's wife answered. "Hi, this is Felix Unger. Nick around?" Felix Unger, Oscar Madison. Why not? Todd and Nick were about as odd a couple as could be.

"Nick's not here."

"Can you give me another number where I might reach him?"

She snarled as if he'd just asked her to donate ten thousand dollars to the Hare Krishnas temple building fund. Todd heard the sound of rustling papers. She rattled off a number. Todd had to ask her to repeat it. She did and he dialed.

"Broward General." It was a woman's voice, cold and unyielding.

"I'm sorry," said Todd. "I must have the wrong number. Is this—" He repeated the number Trish Durham had given.

"Yes, sir. Can I help you?" She seemed to be in a hurry.

"Is there a Nicholas Durham there?"

"Patient, doctor, what?"

Todd hesitated, "Uh, police officer."

"I'll check." She sighed. "What was your name, sir?"

Todd hung up. He drove to Broward General Hospital and, ignoring the signs, parked in a spot reserved for doctors. A woman in a dark suit manned the reception desk. Beside her, a young man in a wheelchair worked at a computer. Todd smiled. "I'm here to see Nicholas Durham."

"Better hurry," said the woman, her hair tied up like it might try to run away if she let it go loose. "Visiting hours are over in twenty minutes."

"Visiting hours?"

"That's right. You know the room number?"

Todd shook his head.

The receptionist typed in Durham's name and gave him

directions to his room.

Todd followed the path the receptionist had laid out for him. The door to Durham's shared room was open. Curtains were drawn around two of the four beds. A gnarly looking Hispanic in twin arm casts looked up hopefully as Todd came in the door. Hope turned to disappointment as the man realized that Todd was neither friend nor foe. Merely nobody. Todd felt a need to apologize for this, but refrained. It wasn't his fault, after all.

The other visible bed was empty, the sheets unmade and dirty. "Nick? Nick Durham?" Todd said quietly. The place smelled of disinfectant and disease. An aura of death and vulnerability hung like an invisible cloak in the air.

Todd hated hospitals.

The Hispanic nodded his chin toward's his right side. The curtain there rustled. Nick's voice called out. "Yeah?"

Todd tiptoed over and pulled back the white drape. Durham lay in bed, a cast up to the hip of his left leg. A stiff collar was wrapped around his neck. "Nick, what happened to you?"

Durham glowered. He urged Todd to pull the curtain shut around them. "Are you crazy? What the hell are you doing here? We can't be seen together. How stupid are you, Todd?"

Todd tapped the thick cast. "Stupid enough, I suppose. Stupid enough to think that you could take care of one doughboy doctor."

Durham's eyes hardened like a couple of apricot pits. "I'm trying to rest here."

Todd paced the tiny, enclosed space. It was warm and he was sweating. "Rest. Must be nice. Know what it's like trying to rest, trying to sleep when somebody is trying to kill you?" He kept his voice low, not wanting Durham's roommates to overhear.

"I tried." Durham's hands lay limp in his lap. He looked like a guy who'd given up on the world.

"What happened, anyway?" Todd fell into a cushionless metal chair against the wall.

"I was tailing your pal, Doug."

Todd stiffened. His fingers curled. "You saw him?"

Durham nodded.

"I knew it. What happened? Did he see you? Did you—" Todd couldn't say the words for fear of being overheard.

"I didn't get the chance."

Todd nodded towards the broken leg. "Because of that?"

"That's right." Durham punched his pillow and leaned forward. "Listen, the guy's clever but not so clever. I've dealt with his type before. He made a common mistake, he frequents certain restaurants. I asked around.

"Wasn't hard to get the info out of his nurses. They don't have much to do with the office closed down except for getting things in order. And that one girl of his, Peg. She likes to talk. She knows Doug inside and out. Probably better than his wife. Anyway, even dead, a guy tends to go where he likes the food."

"But surely the staff at any restaurant would recognize him and it's been in the papers that Doug is supposed to be dead. He'd be taking quite a risk."

"He wore a disguise. Combed his hair different. Wore a

hat. Had a fake moustache."

Todd remembered. The guy in the Bahamas had a dumb-looking moustache. A fake. "What else did you find out?"

"I tailed him awhile. Found out where he's staying. A little dive in Wilton Manors."

Probably paying for it with my money, fumed Todd. "Now what happens?"

There was a smile on Durham's face that Todd didn't like the look of. "Now I close my eyes and get some rest."

"I mean about our friend."

Durham ran a hand along his cast. "Did I mention that I went by my post office box last evening? That's how I got this. Guy tried to run me down. Tried to kill me." His hand stopped on his knee. "Busted in three places. Might never walk straight again."

"That's tough," said Todd. Not that he cared much.

Durham nodded. "The driver of that car was Doug. I told you he was smart. He must have followed me after I left his place." The detective cursed. "I let my guard down. That was stupid. And now I'm paying the price. I picked up my mail and was crossing to my Chevy. The other car came out of nowhere. Only had a second's notice. Lucky he didn't catch me full on. I'd be dead."

No great loss, thought Todd.

"Were there any witnesses?"

"No. Post office was closed for the day. They keep the door to the boxes open. I was the only one there at the time. Except for your friend." He looked at Todd oddly. "Time kind of froze there for a second. That car only feet away, heading straight for me. I thought I was dead for sure. And I could see his face. He was grinning. The bastard was grinning like the devil himself."

Todd's heart seized up. Sonofabitch. "What are you going to do about it?"

"Like I said, I'm not going to do anything about it. I'm going to close my eyes, rest my head on this comfy pillow and recuperate. Wife even brought me some candy." Durham pointed to an open, half-eaten box of chocolates on the bedside table. "Help yourself."

"Listen to me, Nick. We're in this together. If I go down, you go down."

Durham smirked. "I already am down."

"You know what I mean. You've got to do something about Doug trying to kill me. Not to mention about the police trying to pin Caroline's murder on me. We both know Doug did it."

Durham shrugged and popped a chocolate into his mouth. He chewed slowly. "My leg's busted. Forget it."

Todd rose and crossed his arms over his chest. "I'm not paying you."

Durham shrugged again.

Todd struggled to maintain his composure. His world was crashing around him and he was in the center of the 7.8 earthquake, trying to stand his ground. "At least tell the police what you told me."

"What's that?"

"That Doug Freeman is alive. That he is trying to kill me. Like he tried to kill you."

Durham's lips and tongue were stained with chocolate. He looked like a chocolate liquor sucking vampire who'd just sunk his fangs into a chocolate bar corpse. "Not a chance. The doctor might just be able to finger me for my involvement in his little boating mishap."

The detective scratched his neck. "Can't figure out what went wrong there. He must have seen or heard me and jumped ship before she blew."

"If you don't tell them," said Todd, "I will."

Durham pulled at a plastic cord that was twisted in his sheets. "No you won't." At the end of the cord was a white, rectangular call button which he pushed.

A tall male nurse with an inverted triangle for a torso arrived and Todd was asked to leave.

:29

Todd hated it when other people were right.

And Durham was right.

Todd wouldn't tell the police. Even if he did, they probably wouldn't believe him. They'd never take his word over Nick's. Nick Durham was one of their own.

And Todd? Todd was a suspect in an ongoing murder investigation. Not to mention a few other shady dealings that he'd rather the police never find out about. Some things should never see the light of day. Like vampires and unreported income.

But the police were like those stubborn pigs snorting along the countryside of France looking for those rare and elusive truffles, the so-called Black Pearls of Perigord that were so highly prized by gourmands.

Funny he should think of a pig reference. It had to be that damn Mr. Squeals' influence. Great, now a pig was affecting his mind. Like he didn't have enough problems to cope with.

Todd rolled the Chiclet-sized folded bit of paper round

and round in his fingers. At least Durham had acquiesced and given Todd Doug's current address. It just might give him a fighting chance.

He was going to head there now. Wilton Manors. The duplex where Dougie-boy was now hiding out while plotting his sinister deeds.

The beige two-door sedan following him gave him pause. Definitely a woman behind the wheel. That ruled out Doug. Unless the madman had undergone a sex-change operation. Being a doctor, possibly self-performed. Todd ruled out nothing when it came to Deranged Doug Freeman.

The car, a Ford, had been following him since he'd left his office. Worried about the likely tail, instead of driving to Wilton Manors he went to Florida Sunshine Savings and Loan. Gliding through the swinging doors, he espied Holly at her desk going over some dreary looking paperwork with some dreary looking young couple. Probably buying their first house.

Todd couldn't help wondering who the realtor had been. Professional curiosity even in the face of imminent death. It was a curse.

He waited until the couple departed then hurried over. But Holly had noticed him and was scurrying just as quickly away. "Holly!"

She paused near the opening to the counter and lambasted him. "What are you doing here, Todd?"

"I need to see you. Please."

"Go away." She lifted the hinged counter top.

"Please, Holly. I want to apologize."

Her icy eyes stared at him. "Fine. Apology accepted. Now

go away."

Todd froze. That woman by the rack of brochures. That was the woman in the car that had been following him all over town.

"Are you listening to me, Todd?" Holly crossed her arms. Tapped her foot. Clutched her paperwork to her chest.

"Huh? Yeah, listening. I'm listening." He nodded towards the brochures. "Do you know that lady?"

Holly studied the woman. Blue jeans, yellow blouse. Looked like she worked out. Blonde. Cut short. But Todd liked short hair on women. "Why? You want me to introduce you? Caroline's dead and you need a new playmate? You're disgusting."

"No, it's not that." Todd clutched Holly's forearm. "Please, keep your voice down. And don't look. But that woman. She's been following me."

"Oh, please."

"I'm serious. She followed me from my office. She's been following me all around."

Holly stole another look. "Why?"

Todd shrugged. "I don't know. A cop maybe?"

Holly whispered. "The police think you killed Caroline."

"I didn't."

Holly pouted. "I know. At least I think I know. You may be a creep, but I don't think you're a killer."

"Thanks. I'm not. And I'm sorry about Caroline. It was just one of those things. She was feeling low and I just sort of let her seduce me." He hung his head. "I wasn't thinking."

Holly's full red lips moved side to side. "No, you weren't."

"It will never happen again. I swear." He laid a humble hand over his heart.

"I don't know..."

"Listen, Holly. I'm in trouble. Big trouble." Todd decided it was time to lay the cards out on the table. At least most of them—he had to keep a few aces up his sleeve, didn't he? What did he have left to lose anyway? "Is there someplace we can talk?"

Holly nodded and led him to the break room. They had the place to themselves. She pulled a bottle of Perrier from the fridge, dropped into a chair at a long table and sipped.

Todd closed the door and paced. "It's Doug. He's trying to kill me."

"Doug is dead, Todd. Blown up, remember?"

"No, he's not. And he's trying to kill me. He's been trying to kill me for some time now. Since the day I had my checkup, you remember. He gave me five minutes to live and I've been running ever since." She looked dubious. "And Nick. Doug's trying to kill him, too."

"The detective?"

"That's right. Doug tried to murder him, too. Tried to run him over."

"I don't believe any of this." Holly crossed her legs and ran her thumb along the lip of her bottle.

"It's true, Holly. Nick's in the hospital right now, Broward General, with a broken leg. Doug ran him down." Todd laid his hand on Holly's shoulder. "And he killed Caroline. I know he did. And he's trying to frame me for it."

"That shouldn't be hard to do," scoffed Holly. "After all, the police found your body fluids on her nightgown and her body."

Todd winced like he'd been struck with a ball-peen hammer.

"If all this is true," continued Holly, "why don't you go to the police, Todd? Why doesn't Nick go to the police. Heck, he is the police."

Todd sighed. "Nick doesn't want anything to do with it. He refuses to talk. Listen, Holly. . ." This was it. The moment of truth. "I asked Nick to take care of Doug."

She cocked her head. "How do you mean 'take care of Doug'?"

"I asked Nick to see if he could get Doug to lay off me. Stop trying to kill me."

Holly rose. Her face had blanched like a boiled cabbage. "You asked Nick to kill Doug?"

Todd swallowed. "Not exactly. I mean I didn't ask him to murder him or anything. I only wanted him to make Doug leave me alone. But he might have gotten carried away." Todd lowered his voice. "He may be responsible for Doug's boat blowing up."

Holly's mouth turned into a capital O.

"I'm telling you, Holly. That detective's a psycho. Holly?"

Holly's eyes were narrow slits. They reminded Todd of those slits he'd seen in castles visiting France, way up high in the walls. He half-expected to see boiling oil or fast and deadly arrows come shooting out. "You killed Doug."

"No!" He grabbed her hands. "It's not like that at all. Besides, I keep telling you—Doug is alive."

She pulled away and rubbed her wrists. "You can't prove it."

He shook his head. "Maybe not. I don't know whether I can or not. But I do know he is alive and trying to kill me. And if he can't kill me, he's going to see that I go to jail for murdering Caroline, a murder he committed."

Holly was silent.

"It was Doug who attacked me in Nassau. I had some money with me. He stole that, too."

"How much money?"

Todd told her.

Holly whistled. "Where'd you get that kind of cash?"

"Some business deals. Offshore, mostly. With clients like Constantine. I was keeping the money in a safe deposit box on the island. I'd gone there while you were resting and taken the money out to bring back to Florida."

Holly was smiling now. "You're not the most honest guy in the world are you?"

"I try."

"You're going to have to try harder." Holly leaned into him. "For instance, why is Doug trying to kill you, Todd?"

"Why?" Todd tugged his collar.

"Yes, why?"

"For sleeping with Caroline, of course. I told you that."

Holly ran her finger along his shirt buttons. "But you said that Doug's been trying to kill you since the day you had your checkup."

Holly was still smiling but there was something scary in her voice. "But, you also said you'd only slept with Caroline once and that was the night she was killed."

Todd stifled a scream. He'd stepped into an invisible bear trap, one of those big cartoon ones with shark-sized steel teeth. He could feel the triangles of death biting through his ankle. Holly was one rascally rabbit and he was one befuddled Elmer Fudd. He hated cartoons. Seen too many of them as a kid.

Her brow went up. A look of satisfaction passed across her face. She gave him a push. "Goodbye, Todd."

"But—"

"Goodbye." Holly opened the door and disappeared.

Todd stood there a moment, catching his breath. This was not the way this was supposed to go. Not at all. He went back through the rear offices and around the counter. The woman was still there. Sitting in an overstuffed purple chair, reading a brochure about balloon mortgages.

"Looking to buy?" he asked.

She glanced up over her brochure, a look of amusement on her face. "That's right." She had a fluffy head of curly red hair that bounced when she moved and a tiny silver cross dangled from a chain round her neck.

"You're in luck. I'm a realtor. But then," Todd said, his voice hardening like cooling lava, "maybe that's why you've been following me all day?"

The woman uncrossed her legs. "I don't know what you're talking about."

"Of course, you do," said Todd, making no pretense of keeping his voice down. "You've been following me since I left my office. You mind telling me why?"

She glared at him, then slowly stood. She pulled a slim leather wallet from her purse and pulled out her ID. "Det. Wallace."

"I knew it," said Todd, smugly. "What do you want?"

"What I want," she said in a sing-song voice, "is to nail you for the murder of Caroline Freeman."

"I didn't murder Caroline Freeman," Todd said through gritted teeth. "Doug Freeman did."

"Interesting. A dead man kills his wife. That's original."

Todd's face reddened. "Look, detective, I don't care whether you believe me or not. Doug Freeman is alive. He killed his wife and he's trying to kill me. I'm a law-abiding citizen. I didn't kill anybody!"

"Then you shouldn't mind me following you." She faced him down.

Neither said a word. A security guard headed their way. "Everything all right here?"

Det. Wallace's eyes sparkled maddeningly. "Fine. Right, Todd?"

Todd turned on his heels and stomped out.

:30

Surfer Steve was sitting on a bench smoking a Camel beside Carlos the doorman outside the Port Lauderdale building when Todd pulled up. The GT2, polished like a black diamond, sat in front of the building.

Todd parked his mom's Camry beside it. "I see you got your dad's car back."

Steve exhaled a cloud of gray. "Hey, bro'. Yeah, thanks for taking care of her. Pop wants to talk to you."

"Yeah?"

Steve nodded. Carlos discreetly drifted away. "Yeah. About the car." Steve tugged on his cigarette. Blew out another little thundercloud. "And stuff."

"Stuff?" Todd was in no mood for this and said so. "And the police were after me for that little stunt you pulled with the Sebring. That car was a rental. The police impounded it and now I'm stuck with about a twenty thousand dollar bill."

"That's tough, dude. Sorry."

"Just pay me back. Cash. We'll call it even."

Surfer Steve, in a pair of ghastly orange and pink striped

pants and extra-large Ozzfest 2000 T-shirt, shook his head. "No can do. I ain't got that kind of bread, man." He grinned. "We could ask Pop."

Todd sighed. That was the last thing he wanted to do, drag Mr. Brezhinski into his troubles. He needed to stay on the man's good side. A good side that could pay off with a handsome paycheck for himself. Enough to make the twenty G's seem like small change. "Forget it."

Steve grinned. "Cool." He pulled the pack of Camels from his pants. "Want one?"

Todd said no. Damn things reminded him of his mother and his mother reminded him of his charbroiled condo.

"Ready to go?"

Todd frowned. "You mean now?"

"Yeah, I told you my pop wants to see you, dude. He sent me to fetch you. Me and Carlos have been hanging, waiting for you to get back."

Todd climbed back to his feet. It was a long climb. "Fine." He aimed a finger at Steve. "But no side trips. No detours." He glanced at the Porsche. "And no speeding."

Surfer Steve giggled. "You realtors. You're freaks, you know that?"

Mr. Brezhinski was out on the pool deck, seated at a table under an emerald blue umbrella. Dark sunglasses wrapped his eyes into enigmas. He rose as Steve and Todd approached.

"Have a seat, Mr. Jones."

Todd said hello and took a chair that was half in the sun.

"I trust you are well?"

Todd nodded. "Your son said you wanted a word with

me?"

Brezhinski said yes.

"If it's about the land across the street, I'm still working on it."

"Does this imply positive movement?"

"If by positive movement you mean have I secured a deal, the answer is no." Brezhinski's face clouded over. Todd added, "But I'm sure we can work something out, sir. I just need more time."

Brezhinski's fingers played over his glass like a flute. "I see. I would be most disappointed if you let me down."

"Yes, sir."

"But that is not why I called you here today."

"It's not?"

Brezhinski sadly shook his head. "I received a telephone call from the police in Aventura."

Todd forced himself to show no emotion.

"It seems my GT2 was identified as a vehicle of some interest as it was parked outside the home of a Mrs. Freeman who was murdered in that home."

"Mrs. Freeman was a friend of mine. Her husband recently died. I was consoling her. Steve," Todd pointed at Brezhinski's son who was sipping a cola at the bar, "told me I could borrow the car. I didn't want to, but he insisted and—"

Brezhinski cut Todd off. "My son has explained this all to me. There is no need to repeat the story." He leaned across the table. "Let me be blunt."

A squat, chubby woman in a white dress appeared and announced that Mr. Roberts had arrived.

Brezhinski told her to send him out to the patio. A tall,

lanky man in a blue pinstriped suit paced confidently across the deck and Todd followed his steps. There was a leather briefcase in his left hand. His hair was silver and so stiff the breeze couldn't disturb it.

Lawyer, surmised Todd. And he wasn't mistaken.

"This is Lawrence Roberts, my attorney."

Todd half-rose and shook the cool hand that presented itself.

Roberts sat between Todd and Brezhinski. Surfer Steve was shooting baskets at the poolside setup.

"My son also had some trouble the other night. The police in Miami have suggested he may have been involved in some illegal activity of his own that night. He insists this is not so."

Todd maintained a safe silence. No way he was going to bad talk Steve to his dad. That was definitely a no-win situation.

"My son is impetuous and sometimes," Brezhinski paused, as if waiting for his thoughts and words to come together, "acts on impulse. His impulses are not always wise."

Todd could only nod.

The lawyer broke in. "The car was rented in your name. Steve says you loaned it to him and that he'd left the keys in the car while he was in Hollywood having dinner. Unfortunately, he went to a drive through, Taco Bell, and there are no witnesses. Steve explained that he had dinner in his car then went inside to use the restroom. When he came out the car was gone."

Todd had to give Steve credit. It wasn't a bad story at all, as far as fairy tales went. A glimmer of hope appeared like a couple of fused energy particles in the deep recess behind Todd's eyes. He straightened. "Wait a minute," he said, looking at the lawyer. "What night did you say this was?"

"The same night your lady friend was murdered."

Todd smiled. "Then the police are wrong. Steve couldn't have been involved in any drug deal. He was staying at my place."

Brezhinski looked at his attorney and beamed. "I knew it."

"Do you have any witnesses to this?" asked Roberts. "Besides yourself?"

"My mother," answered Todd. "She was there. She's staying with me."

"So she will confirm what you've said here?" The lawyer had pulled a legal pad from his briefcase and was making notes in tiny, near illegible script.

"That's right." Todd called to Steve. "Hey, don't you remember? The other night. You hitched to my place from Taco Bell and spent the night."

Steve smiled. "Like I totally forgot about that." He came up behind his father. "That's right, Pop. Caught a ride with a cute chick from Orlando. She dropped me off at Todd's apartment and I crashed there."

"So Mr. Jones' mother saw you?" said Roberts.

"Mother?" Steve shot a look at Todd who nodded. "Sure, I met her. Cool lady. Real cool."

Robertson rose. "I think this should do it." He snapped his briefcase shut. "I'll be sure to give the police this information as soon as I return to my office." He turned to Todd. "They'll want to confirm this with your mother, of course."

"Of course," repeated Todd. "No problem." He hoped.

The attorney withdrew and Brezhinski held out his hand. "Thank you, Mr. Jones. You've proven quite helpful." He studied Todd a moment. "And resourceful."

"Glad to help," said Todd.

"Thank Mr. Jones, Steve. He's just saved you a lot of grief and me a lot of expense."

Steve high-fived Todd. "Thanks, bro'. I owe you."

"Never mind," said Todd, thinking of the gun and drugs already stashed beneath his mattress—the mattress his mother was now sleeping on. "You don't owe me a thing."

Brezhinski was shaking his head. "But we do. Understand, I still want that land, but after what you've done for my son, perhaps we can work something out."

"The builder, Mr. Constantine, did mention that he'd give you first choice on the lots and a great deal if you were interested in building."

"Did you say Mr. Constantine? Aristotle Constantine?"

"That's right. You know him?"

Brezhinski smiled. "Yes. He's something of a gun enthusiast. Our paths have crossed."

Somehow Todd wasn't surprised. The rich lived in a small world, a place no larger than Pluto. And Thug Peter probably loaded up with diamond-tipped bullets that one of Brezhinski's companies provided.

"Please, ask him to give me a call."

"I'll do that." Todd was all smiles now. Life was good. Things were falling into place. Just like he always knew they would.

"Steve will show you out."

Driving back to Fort Lauderdale, Surfer Steve chauffeuring him, Todd hummed a happy tune. Daydreamin' Boy.

"Thanks again, dude. Thought I might get busted for sure."

"You really ought to watch yourself, Steve. I mean, you've got it made. You've got it all. You're rich. Living in a mansion. Driving fancy cars. The world is yours. You can do anything you want."

Steve shrugged, hands gripping the wheel. "That's the trouble. I don't know what I want. So I look for the kicks, you know?"

Todd did. "Still, you ought to settle down. Find some direction. Maybe go to work for your dad? One of these days those kicks are going to come back and kick you in the ass and you're going to end up dead or in prison somewhere."

Steve said he'd do some thinking. "Lucky break for you that it's Constantine that owns the land across the street from our house. Pop really was mad about somebody building there. But now that he knows it Constantine. . ." Steve's voice trailed off.

"They that close?"

Steve pulled off I-95 onto Broward Blvd. "I probably shouldn't be telling you this, but you're cool."

"Telling me what?"

"Pop and Constantine have done some business."

"Business? What kind of business?"

"Guns, of course."

"I didn't know Aristotle Constantine was a gun dealer, too. I thought he was into real estate and restaurants."

Steve grinned. "The way Pop says it, the guy is selling guns to the Greeks on Crete. Trying to foment some sort of revolt or something. I don't know."

"Revolt?" Todd knew little of politics and revolts. And he wasn't even sure who was running things on Crete. It didn't sound like Steve did either. "How do you know so much about Aristotle Constantine, anyway?"

"Don't you remember?"

Todd shook his head.

Steve pulled up to the curb outside Todd's building. "That time I crashed at your place and Constantine called and I told him to go fuck himself. I told Pop about it. Thought it would give him a laugh. It didn't. He told me Constantine was a client of his and that I should be more respectful. Funny that he should be the one to buy the land across the street from Pop's house."

Yeah, funny, thought Todd. He waved goodbye and headed for the twenty-second floor. But not before chewing out the doorman for letting Holly up with that damn pig.

"Sorry," said Sammy, the new day man, "but she was really insistent. And since she's your girlfriend and everything—"

"Forget it," said Todd. Suddenly he felt bad for ragging on the poor sap. Todd was feeling magnanimous. Life was good, he could afford to be nice.

His troubles were unraveling as if by the hand of magic. Durham was out of the way. And no way he was going to pay him. And now Brezhinski was backing off. Oh, Brezhinski still wanted the land undeveloped, but he'd already shown a crack in his resolve. The trouble had all but disappeared.

And the police would give up on Todd as soon as they saw they couldn't pin the murder on him. His mother would be going home as soon as he found her a new condo in Naples, maybe Marco Island, and she could take fat little Mr. Squeals with her.

Holly would forgive him sometime, wouldn't she?

That left only Doug Freeman. The psycho was still out there, gunning for him. He'd swing by Doug's rental in Wilton Manors after dark. Maybe a solution would present itself.

Todd worked his hands. Was he capable of murder? Could he maybe strangle Doug Freeman the way he was convinced Doug had strangled Caroline?

He pressed the elevator button.

A janitor in a baggy green jumpsuit and matching cap pushed a broom near Todd's feet. Dust balls climbed Todd's shoes.

"Watch it," snapped Todd.

The janitor dropped his broom. A pistol appeared in his hand.

The first stupid thought to pass through Todd's mind was *when did the building begin hiring armed janitors?* His second thought was *this guy looks familiar.* "Doug!" Todd pushed him backward. Doug tripped over the fallen broom and scrambled to his feet.

Todd heard the sound of a gunshot as he ran out the door. Where the hell was the doorman? He squeezed his eyes shut at the sound of the next blast, waiting for the bullet.

But it never came.

He'd slammed into a wall. Todd opened his eyes. The wall was Thug Peter, neatly pressed suit, freshly polished shoes, manicured nails, shiny gun. Peter pushed Todd out of the way. "Move, you idiot! Get out of my way!" he hollered. Peter's gun hand bobbed, looking for its target.

Todd dove for the bushes and poked his head out.

"You can get up," said Thug Peter, thrusting his weapon back into its underarm holster. "Fucker's gone."

Todd pulled himself to his feet. His legs were like jelly he was trembling so bad.

"Who was that?"

"Guy that's trying to kill me."

Peter scowled. "I got that part. What I'm wondering is why?"

"For sleeping with his wife." Todd dusted off his trousers. Bits of ficus had embedded themselves in the fabric. Some kind of ten thousand legged bug was crawling up his leg. He squished it. "You didn't happen to kill him, did you?"

Peter shook his head. "Nah. Not even sure if I hit him."

"Too bad."

"Yeah."

They turned at the sound of sirens. Three squad cars were racing up the drive. Sam the doorman appeared out of thin air, more specifically from behind his stand where he'd been crouching. "I called the police," he said. "Don't worry."

"Gee, thanks," said Todd.

Police spilled from the cars, guns drawn. Thug Peter had raised his hands and Todd thought it judicious to follow his lead.

They were interrogated for what seemed like hours. Both men said they couldn't make out the assailant and Sam the doorman, who'd been hiding throughout the ordeal, backed them up on this. Since Peter thoughtfully had a permit for his gun, the police wrote up a report and left after getting Peter's word that he'd come down to the station later and give a statement. Todd, too.

After they'd gone, Peter said, "You want my advice, Jones?"

"What's that?"

"Stick to single women." He grabbed Todd's elbow and led him to the parked Cadillac ESV that Todd had failed to notice earlier. Though the big-wheeled vehicle was awfully hard to miss being the SUV on steroids that it was.

Constantine was inside. With the engine running. This was his office on wheels. There was practically room for a secretary along with an escritoire, one of those little French desks. It was a blistery sixty degrees or so in the cabin.

"I should have packed a parka," said Todd, sliding across the icy backseat.

"What kind of crap are you up to now?" barked Constantine.

"You saw that?" Todd blew hot air into his hands.

"Of course I saw that." Constantine shook his head. "What's wrong with you, Mr. Jones? Seems like you just can't stay out of trouble."

Amen to that, thought Todd. "So what brings you here, Mr. Constantine?" Todd had a craving for a hot cup of coffee, preferably with a couple healthy shots of Jack Daniels right about now. Didn't this Caddie come with a fireplace, for crying out loud?

"It's those damn lots."

"I think our troubles are over, Mr. Constantine. I was speaking to the man that wanted to buy up the land a little while ago and—"

"Not that," snarled Constantine. He shoved a paper under Todd's nose. "This."

"What's this?"

"Read."

Todd uncrinkled the paper. It was on official City of Boca Raton letterhead. He gaped. "This can't be."

:31

"Environmental impact studies?" Todd mouthed the words like they were typed in some sort of foreign language. "Application to build denied?"

Constantine, despite the chillness of the air, was fuming. He snatched the paper from Todd's hand. "What are you going to do about this, Jones?"

"This has got to be a mistake." Todd squirmed across the leather. Why did it suddenly feel so hot inside? "I personally looked into everything. Approval for the homes and even docks."

Constantine's nostrils flared. "I hold you personally responsible for this, Mr. Jones. I've got a lot of money tied up in this deal. Nothing's going to sour it." His eyes drilled into Todd like titanium tipped bits. "Nothing."

"Yes, Mr. Constantine." Todd grabbed the door release. Locked. "Is that all?"

"A minute, Mr. Jones. I also read in the papers that you're in some trouble with the police."

"It's nothing."

"Nothing? They say you are suspected of murdering a woman."

"It's all a big misunderstanding."

"Huh," snorted Constantine, his body shaking. "A misunderstanding." He waved the wrinkled paper under Todd's nose. "Like this is a misunderstanding?"

Todd sucked in a breath, air so cold his lungs nearly stiffened and practically refused to collapse. "It all started because this nut—he's trying to kill me and—"

Constantine shook his head and waved his hand. "Enough. I do not hear your troubles, Mr. Jones. I am not your mommy. You listen to my troubles and you appease them."

Todd pressed his lips together and nodded. "I'll go down to the city myself. Straighten this whole mess out. Everything's going to be just fine. You'll see."

Constantine pressed the lock release. *Chi-ick*.

Todd pulled the handle. A wedge of hot, humid air fought its way to him. "Oh, I almost forgot. The man who owns the house across the street from your lots. He says he knows you."

"What's this man's name?"

"As I mentioned earlier, Mr. Constantine, it's Brezhinski."

"Brezhinski, Brezhinski." Constantine tapped his long nose. "Yevgeny Brezhinski?"

Todd said yes. "He wants you to call him."

Constantine was actually smiling now. "Well, well. Yev. Didn't know he had a home in Boca. You know, Mr. Jones, with a little luck you just might live to collect a commission."

"Listen, Mr. Constantine. I know I probably shouldn't

ask." Todd gazed out the smoky-glassed window. "But is there anything you can do to help me out with the police? With this murder thing."

Constantine's brow went up and he shook his head. "I steer clear of the police, Mr. Jones. They are not good for business, if you know what I mean."

Todd did.

Todd's mother was on the patio outside the charcoaled guestroom sprawled out on the lounger sunbathing, topless no less. "Must you, Mother?" He tossed a spare towel over her bosom and took a seat.

Mr. Squeals was lying in the sun beside her, snoring like a diesel locomotive. His (was it a he? Todd didn't care to look) big belly moving in and out like a bellows.

"You took down the plastic. You shouldn't have done that. Looks like rain."

"I needed someplace I could get some privacy. Did you know that the neighbors can see onto the balcony off the living room?"

Todd shook his head.

"Well, they can. Woman called and complained. Said her niece and nephew were looking at me. She was mad at me. Me! Is it my fault if the kids are looking at my titties? I didn't ask them to."

Great, now his next door neighbors were mad at him, like they weren't angry enough already about the little fire incident. Now the condo board would have him up on obscenity charges as well.

Not to mention the Caroline Freeman murder. The board

would frown on having a murder suspect as a tenant. Could they force him to sell up and move out? He figured he'd better re-read his condo rules. Where were they?

Then he remembered. Guest room closet, box in the corner. A quick glance told him the state they were in. Ashes. Still damp ashes.

"I need you to do me a favor, Mother."

Mrs. Jones sat up and lit up. "What is it, Todd, baby?"

He explained his meeting with Brezhinski and how his business depended on her providing Surfer Steve with an alibi for Monday night.

"What do I have to do?" She flipped her cigarette over the ledge.

Todd cringed. Now she was tossing her butts off the building to the pool below. What wasn't she capable of? "All you have to do," he said with a sigh, "is say that Steve spent the night here on Monday."

"But that would be lying."

"It's no big deal, Mother. Steve didn't do anything. But he has no alibi. We'd be doing Mr. Brezhinski a huge favor. Could mean a lot of money for me." He turned on the sweet sauce. "I could buy you a new condo. How about a penthouse? Marco Island, Gulf view?" Some place that would allow pigs as pets.

"I don't know. . ." Mrs. Jones was wavering.

"Please, Mother."

Her hand reached down and scratched Mr. Squeals tummy. "You know what I'd really like?"

Todd shook his head.

"I'd like to stay here."

"Of course." Todd smiled. "You can stay as long as you need. I'll contact one of my friends on the west coast. When we find you the right place—"

"No, no, no," she said, taking her son's hand. "I want to stay here." She looked him in the eye. "With you."

Her eyes were seagrape green, like his. An even match any other day of the week. But this time she had him beat. He was in a bind and she knew it. His own mother! Playing hardball!

"You mean you want to move in," he gulped, "permanently?"

Mrs. Jones smiled.

"And in exchange you'll tell the police that Steve Brezhinski spent the night in the condo?"

"That Steve," she said, "such a nice young man. We played rummy and drank greyhounds. I was sorry to see him go."

Todd stood. His knees creaked. Lord, he was getting old, he suddenly realized. Or maybe it was recent events which had aged him beyond the norm. "You've got a deal. We'll get the guest room redone. You can redecorate it however you like."

She looked pleased. "Purple. I like purple. We'll have purple wallpaper."

"Fine, purple. But *we* who? You don't have a boyfriend you're about to spring on me, do you?"

"I'm talking about Mr. Squeals, silly."

Silly me, thought Todd. His own vision included Mr. Squeals roasting in one of those big pits the Hawaiians were fond of cooking with. Instead, he said, "It's a deal. In the meantime, I'd get in if I were you. Looks like rain."

The sky offshore was purple and brown, like a fresh bruise. The temperature had dropped several degrees and the wind was kicking up.

"And get this plastic back up over the busted windows. Otherwise the rain's going to get in. There's some duct tape in the junk drawer in the kitchen."

Like there wasn't enough water damage already from dousing the fire.

"Where are you going?"

"I have to show a property. Be back later."

Mrs. Jones said she'd get right on it.

:32

It was a shabby duplex in a shabby neighborhood. The kind of neighborhood Alvin and his Drugmunk buddies might dwell in if the street rats didn't mind sharing.

Todd had parked at the corner across from a vacant lot strewn with car parts and litter. Coke cans had Pepsi cans beat here by about two to one. Beer cans far outnumbered them both. Fifty to one at least.

Todd turned up his collar. The sun was invisible behind the massive storm clouds which cast an early darkness over everything. The street was quiet, probably because of the weather. There was a foul dankness to the air, garbage and wet mingled with the subtle scent of despair.

Todd looked for the hundredth time at the scrap of paper in his hands. Doug's address. One light was on in the front window of the unit on the left. A shaded forty watt bulb on a rattan table. But the unit on the right was dark. Todd inched closer. That was Doug's apartment.

Todd crossed between the narrow side yard and found a back door with iron bars. He tried the handle. Locked.

Staying close to the wall, he tried the windows. The first two were fastened, but the third gave way. Fortunately there was a thick wall of palmetto palms around the perimeter of the backyard. It wasn't likely that anyone had spotted him.

Todd pushed the window up, braced his hands on the sill and stuck his head through the drapes hoping to hell he didn't get it blown off. Silence greeted him.

Slowly, he slid through the window. It was a bedroom. Lit only by the fading light of outdoors. He fell onto the bed, a narrow twin that squeaked like a frightened guinea pig.

Todd held his breath. Waited for the running footsteps, the follow-up gunshot.

None came.

He rose slowly to his feet. The threadbare carpet was no cleaner than that empty lot across the street. Was this really Doug Freeman's place? Could Durham have been wrong? How could a guy like Doug stand to live in this godawful place, even for a night?

The bedroom door leaned open on bent hinges whose nails barely clung to the doorframe. The apartment was deserted.

An empty McDonald's sack sat abandoned on the kitchen counter. Todd could smell the burgers and fries. A twinge of fear and hunger passed through him. He hadn't eaten since morning.

Someone had been here. And recently. An unfinished cup of soda sat on the uneven kitchen table. He lifted it. There was still some ice melting inside.

Papers were spread out across the table. One in particular caught Todd's attention. It was City of Boca Raton stationary.

That sonofabitch. Doug must have sent that letter to Constantine revoking the building permit. Doug stole or somehow got a hold of some official stationary and typed up that letter himself trying to sabotage Todd's deal.

Todd looked around. There was no sign of a typewriter or a computer. But Doug could have borrowed one or rented one. Even the libraries had them available to patrons.

Todd laid the paper down. There were more important things on his mind. Like his money. It was probably here right now, stashed away someplace a burglar wasn't likely to stumble upon it.

But where? Todd slowly circled the apartment. He looked in the refrigerator. He looked under the lopsided and beer smelling sofa. He ransacked the bedroom and the closets.

Nothing.

"Fuck you, Doug Freeman!"

Someone pounded on the adjoining wall. Todd froze. That was stupid. What if Doug's neighbor came knocking on the door to complain or to see what was going on?

Todd was about to climb back out the bedroom window when he spotted the cracked yellow Bakelite telephone in the corner on the floor, half-buried by yesterday's newspaper. He hit the redial.

"Hello?"

Todd thought the voice sounded familiar. He smashed the receiver against his ear. "Hello. Who is this?"

"This is Charles. How can I help you?"

Charles? The voice suddenly became clearer in his mind. "Charles Gaines?"

"That's right. Who did you say you were?"

"This is Todd, Mr. Gaines. Is Holly there? Can I speak with her?"

"Sorry," said Mr. Gaines. "She's not here. And even if she was, she was very clear that she does not want to talk to you, Todd. I don't know what you did to my little girl, but she's hurt."

"I know. I'm sorry. But listen," Todd said, "I think Holly could be in trouble."

"Trouble?"

"Danger."

"Nothing to worry about. I'm here. My TV's on the fritz so I came over to watch the game. Holly's gone shopping."

"But I think Doug Freeman may be trying to harm her. Kill her even."

"Doug Freeman? He's dead. Besides, why would he want to hurt my Holly?"

Todd sighed. "I can't explain now. It's a long story. When Holly gets home, tell her to stay put. Not to open her door for anyone. I'm on my way."

"Now, listen here, Todd," Mr. Gaines voice was firm, "I told you my daughter does not want to see you. Don't come over here. If you do, I'll call the cops."

"But, Mr. Gaines, if you'd only listen, I—"

Mr. Gaines wasn't listening. In fact, he had hung up on him. Todd threw the receiver against the wall. One more chip in the plaster wasn't going to hurt. Who'd notice anyway?

There was a knock at the front door. Todd quickly climbed through the back window and dropped to the ground. A dog barked in the distance. Black clouds hung over him like the reaching hands of the Devil.

Sticking to the shadows, Todd hurried back to his car.

:33

Todd pounded on Holly's door.

There was no sign of Doug.

Holly answered. She had on a pair of blue jeans and a large gray Victoria's Secret T-shirt. "Go away." She pushed the door in his face.

He stuck out his foot. "Please, Holly. You've got to listen to me. Doug is alive. I think he might be trying to kill you. I was at his house—"

Her face was dark and threatening. "Doug is dead, Todd. If you really think he's alive, then I suggest you see a shrink, because you are losing your mind. Caroline is dead, too, and the Freeman house has been sealed by the police."

"I don't mean that house. I mean the duplex he's staying at in Wilton Manors. He's hiding. He's bent on killing me."

Holly's arms stayed crossed over her chest. "I thought you just said he was trying to kill me?"

"He is. I mean, I think so. I was in his apartment and I pushed the redial button and it was your number and your father answered and I'll bet Doug called before."

"Doug never called here. Would you please leave? Or do I have to call the police?"

Todd waved his arms. "Then it was a wrong number. He could have called and hung up or said he had a wrong number. Did something like that happen?"

She shook her head.

"Maybe your father took the call? Ask him, please."

"He's gone home."

Todd reached for her but she stepped back. "I think I should stay with you tonight, Holly. Just to make sure you're safe."

Holly laughed in his face.

Todd slowly drove home. The old Camry's wiper blades thwacked back and forth pushing water around about as effectively as wet tissue paper. The thunderstorm that had been threatening finally broke through the gates of Earth and came rattling Florida's doors.

With the windows rolled up, the odor of White Shoulders and Camels was near-suffocating. With luck, Todd was thinking, as his eyes struggled to make sense of the blurred landscape ahead, the deadly mixture of gases would kill him and this sorry life of his would soon be over.

But he had no such luck and arrived at Port Lauderdale alive, if not sound. He dropped the car off under the portico and went back up to his apartment. The lights were dim in the lobby. That meant the backup generator was on. Another power outage. The damn electric company never could seem to keep things running.

Fortunately, one of the building's elevators was hooked

into the backup generator. Todd wasn't in a stair climbing mood.

The door to the condo was locked. He fished out his key and opened it up. Mr. Squeals came running, fast, between his legs and out the door and up the hall.

"Hey!" Todd went charging after him. He caught the noisy beast, trapped in the foyer of the corner unit and tossed him back inside. "Damn pig. Mother?"

Todd turned on the dining room lights. The place was otherwise dark but for the flashes of lightning offshore. Mr. Squeals was more agitated than usual and was practically screaming. Todd picked him up under his arm and locked him in the master bath.

"That ought to shut you up." Todd kicked the door out of spite. Being unable to kick the pig, the door made a reasonable surrogate.

Unfortunately, he'd left a scuff mark and a dent. Great, now he'd have to call in the painters. Then again, the gutted guest room needed plenty of work anyway. He may as well go to town, vent his frustration and smash everything.

Instead, he went to the bar and poured himself a scotch. Or three.

The phone rang and he jumped to answer it. The apartment was dark and lonely. Where had his mother gone off to? And with no car. "Holly?" he asked hopefully.

The voice at the other end laughed wickedly. "Sorry, Todd. It's only me."

"Doug!" Todd's glass fell to the carpet, spilling its contents.

"Pretty girl, Holly. Bet she's great in the sack. What do

you think, Todd? You fucked my wife, how about I fuck your girlfriend?" There was another terrible laugh.

"If you hurt Holly—"

"What? If I hurt Holly you'll what, Todd?"

Todd forced himself to calm down. He needed to act rationally. Doug was crazy. If he let himself get crazy, he'd never stand a chance. "What do you want?"

"Well," drawled Doug, "I did want you dead. But all this running and hiding. It wears on a man. I'm tired."

"So stop."

"It's not that easy."

Todd listened to the sound of the rain battering the building. "Maybe I can help. Why don't you keep that money you took from me? Go someplace new, start over."

"I killed Caroline." Doug's voice sounded dead itself.

"I know." It sounded like Doug was crying.

"I killed her," he sniffed. "And the police think I'm dead. My practice is in shambles. There's no way I can start over."

"Sure you can. South America maybe, or the islands. The police will never find you and I'll never tell." Like hell, I won't, thought Todd.

Doug was a long time in replying. "Maybe. Maybe I could do that."

"Sure you can, buddy. Sure you can."

"I couldn't keep your money, though. Not after all I put you through. The least I can do is give it back."

"G-give it back?" Was Doug joking? Would he really give back a quarter million?

"Sure."

"I tell you what," said Todd. "Give it back if you like.

You can leave it downstairs with the doorman."

"I'll do that," said Doug. "It will really make me feel better, lift my conscience. Know what I mean?"

Todd said he did. But what he was really thinking was how totally insane Doug Freeman had become. Had he always been this way? Had he only been hiding it all these years? The guy should have been an actor, not a doctor.

Doug told Todd he would drop the money off, that he would be on his way soon, and hung up.

:34

When he heard the light rapping on the door, Todd turned off the TV using the remote and rose. He'd been watching one of those cooking shows, letting it lull him to sleep with its host's detailed description of pot pie baking.

He yawned. That knocking had to be his mother. Finally, she was home. Who else could it be? He'd called downstairs yet again and told Carlos explicitly to keep visitors out, especially Doug Freeman and Steve Brezhinski. On reflex, Todd looked out the peephole, nonetheless.

Doug Freeman!

Dressed in stained brown trousers and a long-sleeve blue shirt and work boots, his hair wet and clinging to his head like a giant limp paramecium. He had more hair than he should, too. A toupee. But no goofy lip hair this time. Apparently Doug had given up the mustachioed look. In his hands, Doug clutched a navy blue knapsack by the straps.

Todd slowly edged away from the door. He picked up the phone and dialed Holly's number. It rang and rang. Doug knocked again. Louder.

"Holly, Holly. Pick up," muttered Todd. He heard a click and talked fast. "Holly, it's me, Todd. Don't hang up. Please!"

She sighed audibly. "What is it now, Todd?"

"It's Doug. He's here. Right now. Outside my door and he wants in."

"Really, Todd. You're insane. Completely insane. You're having a nervous breakdown. Why don't you just—"

"Holly," Todd cried through gritted teeth, "listen to me for God's sake. Doug Freeman is standing in the hall, dripping wet. I am not lying. And I am not hallucinating! Get over here and see for yourself!"

"Is this the best that you can do?"

"Holly—" The dial tone buzzed in his ear like a wayward yellowjacket looking for the exit. Todd turned. The door handle had rattled.

Todd approached the door. He looked out the peephole once more. Doug was still standing there. His clothes soaked through. A smile on his face. Whistling cheerfully, like he was presenting himself at the door to sell Girl Scout cookies rather than to commit cold-blooded murder.

"Doug," said Todd, raising his voice to be heard through the thick door, "what are you doing here?"

Doug held up the backpack. "Thought I'd bring you your money personally. Show you how sorry I am about everything." He peeled the zipper and tilted the bag towards the peephole. "See?"

Todd saw. Inside was cash. Lovely, green cash. His cash. Todd's hand move slowly to the doorknob. Was it safe to let Doug in? Maybe if he opened the door just enough to get the backpack? Todd's fingers turned the thumb lock. Damn.

Money. Money was his weakness. His million dollar Achilles heel.

Doug must have heard and understood the sound because the next thing Todd knew, Doug was in the foyer. Waving the backpack like a pendulum.

"How did you get past the doorman?"

"Nice guy. But doorman gigs don't pay all that well. I bribed him with a couple hundred. Hope you don't mind, but I didn't have the cash myself. I'm afraid I had to dig into your stash. In fact, I had to spend a bit of it the past few days on essentials. Sorry."

"No problem," said Todd. He reached out to take the backpack but Doug held it at arm's length.

"Not so fast."

"What?" Todd couldn't take his eyes off the dripping pack. He was like a hungry dog eyeing a sirloin.

"Aren't you going to offer me a drink?"

"Huh?" Todd watched as Doug crossed to the bar. "Oh, sure." Todd passed behind Doug and stepped behind the bar. "Scotch all right?"

Doug's right arm came up and Todd flinched. A sharp pain in Todd's shoulder erupted like a miniature volcano. Todd twisted. Doug was clutching a knife in his hand that looked about as big as him.

The only thing bigger than the knife was the stupid-ass grin on Doug Freeman's face. "God, you're pathetic, Todd."

The knife bounced in his hand. The other waved the backpack full of money. Todd's money. "Did you really think I was going to let you go. Let you live, keep all this money?" Doug waved the bag under Todd's nose.

Todd suppressed a scream. His shoulder was afire now and his eyes had watered over. It was like looking at Doug from underwater. "You're crazy."

Doug seemed to find this amusing. "Maybe I am. Maybe I'm not. But you shouldn't have screwed with me. You should not have slept with Caroline. And you shouldn't have gotten me mixed up in your stupid real estate deals."

Doug was shaking his head. "Think you're such a know it all, don't you, Todd? Well, you're not. You're a stupid little, uneducated shit." He took a step toward Todd who was trapped behind the bar. "And you're going to die."

The front door rattled. Doug turned. Todd leapt over the bar, fighting the pain in his shoulder. Blood, his blood, ran over the wool carpets. Doug lunged for him and Todd kept him at bay with a chair.

The door opened. It was Holly. Still wearing what she'd had on when he'd been by her house, with the exception of the Winn-Dixie bag that no doubt covered her head to keep her hair dry.

"Holly!" cried Todd. "Watch out!"

She stood there, an expression of shock on her face. She pulled the plastic bag off her head. "Doug? You are alive!"

Holly turned to Todd. "What on earth is going on? I thought I'd come over. I was so afraid you'd really gone crazy. I found Carlos downstairs. He's dead. I called the police." Her face went from Doug to Todd and back again. "I thought you were dead?"

"Not as dead as the both of you are going to be." Doug grabbed Holly's arm and twisted. She kicked him in the crotch and he screamed, throwing her against the wall. Todd heard a crunch as her forehead glanced off the wall. She collapsed like a broken doll.

"Give it up, Doug. You heard Holly. She's called the police."

"Maybe. But they're going to be too late to save you, asshole." Doug ran at Todd.

Todd threw the chair at Doug and missed. Todd screamed. Doug was on him now. Todd struggled to keep the long, wicked blade from his skin, but his shoulder was weak and he'd lost too much blood. He couldn't hold Doug off much longer.

Out of the corner of his eye, Todd saw Holly coming around. There was an ugly red lump on her forehead that was growing quickly. She dove at Doug's feet and he crumpled. But he jumped back up and growled like a wounded bear.

Todd had fallen. Doug's knife had dug into his right thigh and it was spurting like a mini-geyser. Shit. He was going to die in a puddle of his own blood and Doug was going to kill Holly and there was nothing he could do about it. "Run, Holly!"

She nodded and scrambled to her feet.

Doug let go of Todd and said, his voice harsh and rough as sandpaper, "I'm going to kill her first just so you can watch. Then it's going to be your turn." A brilliant flash of white, a bolt of nearby lightning lit Doug's face. He looked like a deadly phosphorescent ghoul.

Todd cried out as he put weight on his injured leg and raced to save Holly. She'd run into the burnt-out guest room with Doug on her heels. Todd could hear Mr. Squeals crying insanely from the bathroom. The storm and the fighting must have pushed the beast over the edge. That pig sounded as berserk as Doug.

And that's where Todd found them, Doug and Holly, locked in a mad embrace. Doug's knife was at her throat. The room was soaked. Rain swept through unimpeded. Todd's mother had never put the plastic back up over the busted sliding glass doors like he'd asked her.

The floor was soaked. The black plastic flew in sheets like antimatter ghosts. A huge blanket of black plastic covered the floor, catching and holding the rainwater. Todd slipped in a foot of water and slid into Holly and Doug. Doug lost his grip and the knife splashed to the ground.

Todd grabbed Doug with his good arm and tried to get a bear hold on him. "Go," he shouted over the din of the storm. "My room! Under the mattress!"

Holly nodded and flew from the room.

Doug roared in anger and threw Todd off. Todd tumbled out onto the balcony. Cold rain soaked him to the bones, insinuated itself inside his wounds. Doug picked his knife out of the wet muck of the gutted guestroom floor and came stalking.

Where are you, Holly? worried Todd. Where are you?

Todd took a step back and slipped. His back bouncing off the rail. It was a long way down. Why the hell didn't he get a unit someplace closer to the ground? Like the first floor?

"Todd? You here, honey? Mr. Squeals?"

Doug looked to the bedroom door. "Mommy's home," he sneered. "Guess I'll have to take care of her, too."

Todd tried to shout but his voice failed him. Doug lashed

out and Todd dodged to the left. But this game of dodge ball wasn't going to last long.

A strip of plastic blew into Doug's face and the hand holding the backpack rose to tear it away.

Todd was wondering if he could manage to squeeze past Doug in all the commotion when the sound of a rampaging Mr. Squeals filled the room, drowning out even the storm. The pig burst into the room full throttle. Little legs flailing. Doug pawed at the plastic, oblivious to Mr. Squeals.

But Mr. Squeals was not oblivious to Doug Freeman. With a snarl, he plowed into Doug. The backpack splashed to the ground. Mr. Squeals' razor sharp teeth bit into Doug once, twice. Doug shouted. He kicked. Mr. Squeals was tossed back towards the charred remains of the bed.

Doug teetered, off-balance. The wind swirled around him. Gusting. The rain pushing like fat molecules. Doug fell back, arched over the railing.

"Todd, help me!" Doug grabbed for the billowing remnants of the curtains.

Todd staggered towards the sliding door. Mr. Squeals was getting set for a second charge.

The curtain tore and the rod bent, leaving Doug suspended half over the rail. But only for a moment.

As Mr. Squeals mounted his second attack. The curtain rod broke loose from the drywall, caught in the doorframe for a mere second before bending and giving way.

Doug screamed. His hands scrambling for the guardrail and finding only air.

Thank you, Mr. Squeals.

:35

Everything went quiet.

At least that's how it seemed to Todd. Mrs. Jones stuck her head through the door. "What the devil is going on in here?" She clapped her hands and Mr. Squeals jumped into her arms, bowling her over, licking her face.

"Who locked Mr. Squeals in the bathroom?" Mrs. Jones rubbed her nose against his snout. "You poor baby."

Holly ran into the room.

Those brown shapes circling all around her. . .were those cops?

"What's happened, Todd, honey? Oh, dear. I forgot to put up the plastic, didn't I." Mrs. Jones squinted. A cigarette burned in her mouth.

Todd stood there. Had his ears stopped working? Doug Freeman was out there. Somewhere far below. Oh, the neighbors were just going to love this. A human pancake soiling their pool deck.

"Todd? Todd, honey?"

Holly waved her hand in front of his face. "Todd?"

It was like he had two big seashells glued to his ears and all he could hear was the ocean. Maybe he'd lie down awhile. Take a snooze.

Todd woke with the warm sensation of a tender hand in his. He jiggled his fingers and squeezed. "Holly?" He open his eyes, groggy and slow.

"Hey, bro'. " Surfer Steve was all smiles. "You're awake. Finally." Steve pulled his hand away and sucked soda from a can with a straw. "Must have been some dream you were having."

Todd leaned forward on his elbows. "Where am I?"

"Hospital. Broward General." Surfer Steve was looking resplendent in baggy orange shorts and a purple muscle shirt. "I take back everything I ever said about realtors. You're one badass mother."

"What are you doing here?" Todd looked around the room. The bed beside him was empty. A vase of flowers sat on his bedside table. There was a card but he was too tired to look at it. His right shoulder and arm were sore and he discovered he couldn't move them, or his leg.

"Constantine told Pop. Not to mention you made the paper." He tapped his fingernail against a copy of the Sun-Sentinel. "We were all quite concerned about you, dude. You got yourself messed up pretty good. How'd you ever get mixed up with such a psycho?" Steve slapped Todd's bandages. "But the doc says you're going to be fine. Just fine. Have you up and surfing in no time."

Todd rolled his eyes. Look who was calling who psycho. As for the surfing—not in this lifetime. Oh well. At least the kid had cared enough to visit. "Thanks for coming."

"No prob, bro'."

Todd fell against his pillow. "I don't suppose I've had any other visitors?"

"Girlfriend's waiting right outside, dude." Steve stood and winked. "But I'd lay off the heavy lifting awhile, if you know what I mean?"

Todd said he did. Steve disappeared and Holly came through the door a moment later, closing it firmly behind her. Holly's face was half-swollen and bandaged and she looked tentative, unsure of herself, clutching her purse for comfort and support.

Todd sat up. "You okay?" His hand tentatively touched her bandages as she leaned over him.

Holly nodded, sat beside the bed. "You should be taking it easy."

"It doesn't get any easier than this," Todd said with a smile.

"You know what I mean."

"Yes. I know what you mean." Todd reached out with his left hand and took hers. "Thanks for coming."

Holly nodded. "I wanted to let you know that I've got your money in a box at my office. It'll be safe there until you pick it up."

Todd frowned. "The money doesn't seem all that important now."

Holly fingered the card on the flowers. "Hope you like the flowers."

"They were from you?"

"Seemed like the thing to do." She looked embarrassed.

231

"You did save my life, after all."

Todd didn't know what to say. Besides, if it wasn't for his screwing up Holly would never have been in danger in the first place. But why remind her.

"The police have closed their investigation into Caroline Freeman's murder."

"They have? That's good news."

She agreed. "They think Doug faked his own death so that he could kill his wife. They figure he'd gone nuts and was going to kill you next. For sleeping with his wife," Holly added softly.

"He'd have succeed if Mom hadn't let Mr. Squeals out. I'm going to have to revise my opinion of the beast. Especially since he and Mother are going to be staying with me permanently."

Todd squeezed that thought out of his head simultaneously squeezing Holly's hand. "I'm glad you're okay."

Holly pulled her hand away and undid the clasp of her purse. "I brought you something."

"Oh?"

She nodded. "I found this under your mattress." She laid the gun on her lap. Surfer Steve's gun. The one the kid had given Todd along with the baggy full of marijuana.

"Took you long enough."

"Sorry. It's a big mattress."

"King-sized," Todd said with a silly grin. He turned serious. "What are you doing with it here?"

Holly shrugged. Her other hand came out with a plastic bag. "I found this, too." She giggled. The bag half-full was now half-empty.

Holly was mad.

Holly was high.

Todd was in trouble.

He talked fast. Laid out his best smile. "Listen. I'm sorry, too, Hol. I'm sorry for everything. If there's any way I can convince you to take me back?"

"I don't know, Todd." There was no give in her eyes. No give at all.

"Please, Holly. I am so sorry. I know I've been really stupid and I've done some terrible things. Made some mistakes.

"But I'm a changed man now." Todd sighed. "If only there was something I could do to change your mind. Show you I've changed. If you'd only give me a chance—"

She cocked her head. Her pupils bounced on their heels like imps. "Convince me."

Todd froze. He looked at the gun.

Holly was aiming the fearsome black thing at his face with a single, steady hand. She turned her wrist and looked at her watch. "You've got five minutes—"

Also available from Beachfront

MURDER IN
ST. BARTS and
DEATH OF A
CHEAT

Gendarme
Charles Trenet
crime novels

Available in hardcover, trade paperback and Ebook editions

An exciting new series by the critically acclaimed author of
the Tony Kozol mysteries. Murder and romance fill the air on
the exotic island of St. Barts in the French West Indies...

"It would be hard not to like Murder In St. Barts.
The dialogue, the humor, and the sarcasm give us all
something to enjoy." I Love A Mystery

"Trenet is a well-developed, likable character, and the novel
offers an absorbing mystery set in the exotic playground of
the rich and famous. An entertaining new series..." Booklist

"George and the Angels" is intriguing, funny, and plays with notions of reality in ways that bend your mind. It's both a romp and a quest through a world that may or may not be real, with a quirky protagonist who may or may not be crazy. So pull up a chair and get lost for an afternoon!"
TJ MacGregor, 2003 Edgar Award Winning Author

Available in hardcover, trade paper and Ebook

"Glenn Meganck's George And The Angels is an outstanding novel about George Richard's terribly mundane, tedious, and seemingly aimless existence...A truly timeless and well-crafted story of one man's decision to create his own fate in life and pursue even the most disillusioned dreams, George And The Angels is very strongly recommended and entertaining reading." –Midwest Book Review

"A very good read." –Janwillem Van de Wetering

"If the metaphysical interests you, this story will too." – Bookviews

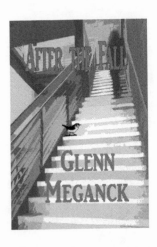

After The Fall by Glenn Meganck
Available in hardcover, trade paper and Ebook

"After the Fall" is a strong pick for general fiction collections and for those looking for novels surrounding the pain of loss." Midwest Book Review

...Meganck does a splendid job in immediately capturing one's attention...Meganck entertains the reader by introducing a wise-talking bird into the life of Jeff. Using humor through conversations with the bird lightens the sadness that the reader has been experiencing up to this point. The author has the reader re-thinking what defines sanity. The bird becomes an intricate part in the rebuilding of Jeff's fractured life. The reader will find this book interesting not only because it is well-written, but also because it offers life lessons on how to pick yourself back up, and shoulder through grief, anger and despair after suffering tragedies that could happen to anyone. Everyone is capable of finding his/her way back and there is no set way of doing this; Jeff's "therapy" happens to be a "crazy bird."

Public and academic libraries looking to add an entertaining, general fiction book to their collections would make a great start with this book. Tennessee Library Association

Look for upcoming Beachfront releases by featured authors including Marie Celine, Nick Lucas, Glenn Meganck, Elmer Joyce, J.R. Ripley and more!

All titles are available (or coming soon) in hardcover, trade paperback, and Ebook editions

Beachfront Entertainment

"Independent Art for Independent Minds."

Beachfrontentertainment.com

Made in the USA
Lexington, KY
02 August 2014